MARCHWOOD

A COZY FANTASY NOVEL

BY

R.A. LORENSEN

MARCHWOOD

A COZY FANTASY NOVEL

BY

R.A. LORENSEN

Lawrence House Publishing is an independent publisher of fantasy based in the American northlands.

R.A. Lorensen is a writer from the Upper Peninsula of Michigan.

Genre: Fiction, Cozy Fantasy for Adults and Young Adults

Mild tobacco and alcohol references are found in this book.

If you like this book, find more at: RALorensen.com.

DEDICATION

To anyone in need of a good, wholesome story.

May your paws be warm and your fires be steady.

Good luck out there.

- R.A. Lorensen

TABLE OF CONTENTS

PART ONE

CHAPTER 1

Nova the red squirrel took a long, slow drink of the warm Valerian root tea that had been steeping on her oaken end table for about half an hour. She brewed the tea in a glazed, clay mug that showed deep tones of coppery clay, burning reds, and spatters of gold and orange. It was about ten o' clock in the morning, not too early, nor too late, and a warm springtime breeze blew in through the open window of her tiny, stone home in Riverbank Village.

She breathed in a smooth, calm breath of the fresh May breeze, and the scent of wildflowers—purple bellflower, marsh marigolds, and blazing stars—mingled with the lemongrass and Valerian root notes of the wide mug of tea that she held in her paws. She smiled, and breathed out calmly and relaxedly. The angle of the sun was just shifting from the glow of morning to the brighter white of the later morning, and the light danced in through the window with the shadows and playful dance of the leaves in the trees and boughs of the tall pines that formed the canopy above her tiny house.

She had prepared a small sandwich to go with her tea. The bread was a hardy brown loaf, freshly baked in the early morning, and spread with an even, thin layer of almond butter. The sandwich was cut in half, diagonally. Of course, the red squirrel then lifted her footpaws and rested them on a comfy stool. As she rested her paws, the sunlight still danced through the leaves and shone in through the windows as the spring breeze gently shook the branches of the high, overhanging elms and hornbeams, and hackberry and hickory.

"Nothing could disturb such a tranquil and peaceful morning," she thought, "and nothing shall."

Nova lived deep in the forest of Marchwood, where there lived the inhabitants of a quiet village that was home to animals from many different walks—and paws—of life. The red squirrels, gray squirrels, chipmunks, porcupines, and red rabbits of the forest fled many years ago from a wildfire in the Eastern Woods, and so came to settle in a place they named Riverbank Village, nestled just on the edge of the River Reed. But that was centuries ago, by their reckoning, and far out of mind. So in the peaceful groves near the River Reed, they built tiny homes made of stone, and built a sturdy wall surrounding their village, and there they lived in peace for as long as the munks (*chipmunks*, that is) could keep record.

But just as Nova was so perfectly settled in, she heard someone whistling a pleasant melody, and then heard a rustling and swishing in the grass as someone approached her porch in Riverbank Village, and knocked on her wooden door. *Knock, knock, knock!* Three times she heard the woody, familiar sound of a friend at the door. Nova was not entirely surprised—she had half expected a visitor, as it was no strange occasion for a friend to visit of a morning hour and stay late into the afternoon, sometimes bringing an instrument or an old scroll or a poem to talk about. Nova loved, above all else, to be at home with a good story, an ancient song, or a curious history to consider, especially with a friend, and especially with a good cup of warm Valerian tea.

"Hello, Nova! Are you in there?" Nova recognized the voice of a friend.

"Yes, I'm coming! Just a moment, dear."

Standing in the doorway, looking a bit excited, was the red rabbit Juniper. She scratched her ears and wriggled her nose

15

with happiness at seeing her friend. But there was a look of worry in her eyes.

"You see, Nova," Juniper began, "Rudbeck is stuck in the hollow of a great spruce tree, just outside the village walls. He was climbing up to take a look inside the hollow, but now he can't get down. I don't suppose you could help, what with being such a good climber and all?"

Nova wasn't at all bothered by the request, and grabbed her moss-green cloak that was hanging up on a peg by the side of the door. It was not an unusual thing for a villager to request Nova's assistance in such a task as this, as she was an excellent climber, and among the quickest of the squirrels who lived in the village.

"Let's go, right away! Oh wait," Nova said, and took the sandwich off the plate. She gave one half to her friend. "We'll want a littele snack for the trail, I suppose."

At that moment, her left ear twitched, and with a sense of instinct, she grabbed her shortsword in its sheath and slung it around her shoulder. Then she grabbed her favorite green wool cap that fit just right, with two holes she had cut herself at just the right angle for her pointy ears. She loved the way it fit just right.

"You never know," she said to herself, adjusting the shortsword, and stepped outside into the warming sun.

In those days, it was not altogether uncommon for the inhabitants of Riverbank Village to leave the walls of their cozy, little town for a walk in the woods. An arch was built at the western edge of the wall, and a volunteer crew of gatekeepers rotated their watch, though they had mostly fallen out of training in those days. It was understood to be an honorary position, and came with a supply of good snacks and plenty of time to doze off or read a book. There wasn't much work to do for a watcher-on-the-wall, not in those days.

Chordy was a stout, young, large-nosed porcupine with a handsome face and big, black eyes. He sat in a wooden chair with his feet resting on the battlement, on top of the wall. Chordy took his post as gatekeeper and watcher-on-the-walls more seriously than most of the villagers, and volunteered as often as he could to have his name in the lists, longing for adventure in the outside world and dreaming of greater glories that the quiet village life couldn't provide. Still, he was content dreaming and watching. When he saw Nova and Juniper approaching, he stood up, fixed the shako cap on his head, and looked out over the battlements into the woods beyond.

"Good day, friends! Fine day for a stroll in the Marchwood. Everything looks clear, from here. No news today, no news. You know what they say, though? No news is good news!" Chordy stamped his poleaxe down on the wall-walk where he stood, looking down at the red squirrel and the red rabbit. "When I'm older, I'll go off adventuring all the time, I 'reckon. Just on a day like today. Great day for an adventure!"

"Well, I suppose you'll be so kind as to open the gate for us, then!" Nova called up.

"I suppose you're right! Where's my manners?" Chordy chuckled, and jogged down the stairs from the wall-walk to the ground, and helped the two raise the massive drawbar that held fast the gate.

"Good day! May your paws be warm and your fires be steady!" Chordy shouted out after them, which was at that time the polite thing to say when anyone left Riverbank Village to venture off into the wider Marchwood, especially if they intended on being away for a while.

Chordy shut the gate to the village, and watched Nova and Juniper disappear into the depths of the Marchwood, chatting and laughing as they went.

CHAPTER 2

Rudbeck the field mouse was indeed stuck in the hollow of an old spruce tree. He had climbed up an enormous, ancient spruce upon which had grown myriad shelf mushrooms, like natural steps leading up the trunk of the tree. He had intended on investigating the hollow for the thrill of some personal gain —supposing, perhaps, that there could be ancient silvers, or a forgotten scroll, or some good sap or honey, or some other treasure—but the last of the fungi broke off underneath his foot and fell down to the forest floor, and the sequence of mushroom steps was broken. Rudbeck the mouse was quite stranded up in the hollow of the tree.

"Up here! I'm up here!" Rudbeck cupped his paws to his mouth as he yelled down at Nova and Juniper. He saw the red squirrel and the red rabbit cheerily walking together. "Have you come to rescue me?" The little field mouse didn't seem too shaken, though he had in fact been stuck in the hollow of the tree for the entire night. He had made himself cozy, sleeping on his backpack, and drawing up a few fresh, green leaves to cover his body in the chilly spring night.

Juniper looked up at the tall spruce. "It's a long way up. I'm surprised he made it as far as he did, up there." Juniper the rabbit wiggled her ears and looked worriedly at her friend.

"It doesn't look bad at all. I see he's quite cozy up there, as it is. But this is short work for a squirrel." Nova unslung the shortsword from her back and handed it to Juniper. "I'll just climb right up!"

Nova scampered up the side of the spruce tree in a whirlwind, scrambling up the bark, then hopping on the mushroom steps, then swinging from a branch and running up its length. She was an expert climber and was always ready to test her climbing abilities.

Rudbeck was surprised when Nova jumped right into the hollow of the tree next to him. "Well, did you find what you were looking for up here?"

Rudbeck, shaking off his surprise, shrugged his shoulders. "Just this old nest, and some feathers," he said. "Might make for good bedding if you stuffed them in something. They make me sneeze, though. Dusty old things." Rudbeck looked around to the back of the hollow, then scratched his head. "You know, I did find this old note. You like books and old scrolls and bits and bobs like that, don't you? I was never much for book learning. Maybe you can make sense of it."

Rudbeck reached into an interior pocket of his long, red cloak, and produced a tattered, rolled up scroll of old parchment. He unrolled it, but the language was unfamiliar to them. The writing looked like runes, more stamped than penned, as if they had been pressed into the parchment with an edge or an old, stone tool. The ink was a deep red, almost purple, as if the ink had been made from the mash of a strange fruit.

"Yes, I do enjoy a good mystery. This looks quite interesting. Do you mind if I take it with me back home and see if I can make sense of it? I'll treat you to some tea and you can tell us about your night in the hollow. Quite the daring adventurer you've become, Rudbeck. Yes, you can tell me all about it. I have some fresh brown bread and a good, mature white cheddar walnut cheese and early lettuces back at home. Fancy a little lunch?"

Rudbeck was indeed very hungry, for he had not eaten all through the night that he was stuck in the tree hollow, and was just about to express his gratitude, when suddenly they both heard a wild yell of surprise from below.

"*Eeeee-yaaaaaah!*"

Nova hurried to the edge of the tree hollow and looked down below at the forest floor. Juniper was holding aloft the shortsword and swinging it over her head, as a whole score of vicious looking toads in iron armor, black capes, and shields and black banners were circling around her.

"Get back, get back, all of you!" Juniper yelled, as she clumsily swung the blade in a wide arc over her head.

"Hurry, come with me," Nova shouted at Rudbeck, and he hopped on her back. Nova tucked the ancient scroll into her cloak pocket and secured Rudbeck on her back, and hopped from branch to branch down to the forest floor to help her friend.

Rudbeck jumped off of Nova's back and unsheathed a bone-handled dagger he had tucked into his belt. He waved it in front of him and gave a menacing look at the pack of toads. Nova picked up a fallen branch and held it in her paws, ready to strike.

The toads stepped back away from Juniper, and went silent. They seemed to blink their dark, black eyes all in unison, as they stared at the field mouse.

Before anyone could act, the toads hopped straight at Rudbeck and a particularly big one slung the field mouse over his shoulder. "*Brinnnng* 'em," they croaked. "*Brrrrinnnng* 'em," they croaked again. Rudbeck tried to wriggle free but the toads were moving at a lightning pace, hopping madly through the woods. Nova tried to run after them as they disappeared to the north, but she couldn't keep pace. Juniper grabbed Nova by the shoulder.

"Wait! We can't fight them all alone. We need help. Let's get back to Riverbank Village, and quick as can be!"

The two friends gave each other a knowing look, and they ran as fast as they could back to Riverbank Village.

CHAPTER 3

Nova and Juniper ran as quickly as their footpaws could carry them on the path through Marchwood forest back to Riverbank Village. They saw the high stone walls growing larger and larger as they sped along the dirt path, kicking up a dust cloud behind them. Chordy the gatekeeper spotted them a long way off, and opened the gate in their advance.

"What news, are you being followed?" He shouted, as Nova and Juniper approached.

"No, Rudbeck's been captured by a band of toads! We need help!"

Chordy grabbed his poleaxe and ran down the steps from the battlements. He shut the gate after them as the squirrel and the rabbit skidded inside the village.

"We'll ring the bell in the Meadow Tower. Let's go," Chordy panted, and joined in with the red squirrel and the red rabbit as they sprinted up the hill to the center of the village.

There, in the middle of Riverbank Village, was the old gathering hall, with its maplewood floors and moss-green painted siding and large bell tower. Inside the gathering hall were tables laid out for hundreds, and the animals of the village could always come to the hall and find a hot bowl of turnip and potato stew, a tasty beverage, and good conversation. But on this warm afternoon it was mostly empty, as the three young villagers clambered up the stairs to the bell tower and rang the great bell again and again, pulling on its old, finely woven rope.

The bell in Riverbank was, in those days, only rung on festive occasions—to usher in the new year, the new moon, the changing of the seasons, and on feast days and celebrations—but the villagers could hear the urgency in its clanging and clattering and quickly came out from their homes and huts and burrows and filtered into the gathering hall at the center of the village at the top of the hill.

Squirrels both red and gray, mice large and small, rabbits and hares, porcupines, and chipmunks in monkish attire filtered into the gathering hall, and it quickly filled with the clamor and cacophony of squeaks and voices and confusion.

Nova, Juniper, and Chordy quit their ringing and descended down the steps from the bell tower into the main gathering hall and looked out on the crowd.

A sagely, elder chipmunk with his hands clasped in front of him looked up at the youngsters. "And pray, what is the meaning of this, my friends? Is there some trouble on this fine spring day?" He did not seem at all irate, but genuinely perplexed at the commotion. Days in Riverbank were spent in gardening, harvesting, cooking, baking, brewing, and making music and merry more than anything else. Few would ever suspect that such mischief as a wild band of toads stalking around in the woods would ever disturb their day.

"Rudbeck has been captured by a band of toads, and we need to hurry. They've run off with him into the deeps of Marchwood," Nova exclaimed, trying to calm her quavering voice.

An uproar of voices filled the gathering hall and reverberated off the walls. "Why, there haven't been toads in these parts in ages," one of the monks remarked, looking at his brothers and sisters in perplexity.

"There's been trouble afoot and I've warned ye' all about 'et," a grumpy old mouse with a long, gray mustache muttered. His companion, a lean and sinewy old mouse in a uniform and broad cap, nodded gravely, "Aye, in my youth there were toads about these parts, and we had to put up a good fight. They still live to the north in the black castle. I'm too old, now, you know, to bother with 'em. Better leave it to the youngsters. But they're untrained! They haven't known hard times like we did." An even elder chipmunk nudged the mustached mouse in the ribs gently, "You exaggerate, of course. We've had peace for decades. You exaggerate!"

An infant mouse started sobbing, and a hare in a royal blue wool shirt with gold buttons slammed a wooden tankard on a table, calling for ale and arms. "To the armory, to the armory! It's war, it is! Shields and swords, my friends! Shields and swords!"

Finally, amid the commotion, the sagely, elder chipmunk— who was named Father Holbrook and who held a high position among the Order of the Munks, the chipmunk sages who lived and studied in Riverbank and kept the libraries and archives in good order—stepped up onto a wooden chair and held out his hands, calmly saying, "Silence, everyone, please. Let's calm ourselves. Let the poor young squirrel have her say. She needs her help, and we must help as much as we are able.

Tell us more, Nova, about young Redbuck and what transpired today." The villagers quieted themselves and listened carefully.

Nova thanked the elderly sage and relayed the story of what had transpired in the Marchwood outside the walls of Riverbank—how Juniper had come to her home that morning, and how the two had left the gates just after ten o' clock, and how they came upon Rudbeck in the hollow of the great spruce tree, and then, finally, how the score of toads in iron armor with black capes and spears had encircled Juniper, and then captured Rudbeck the field mouse. The villagers listened carefully, captivated by every word. Indeed, it had been a long time since bad luck and unwelcome forces had been in the works anywhere near their peaceful and sleepy village. They had become so accustomed to a simple life of steady labors, peaceful relaxation, and well-earned rest, that they were more likely to forget about the outside world altogether than to dwell on its going-ons.

"Surely some evil is afoot in the world again, I say," the mouse with the mustache remarked. "These are changing times."

"We don't know anything, yet. All we know is that a pack of toads has taken our Rudbeck. We must send a search party at once, and form up our forces to defend our walls, in case there are more of these toads about in the Marchwood. We can't be too careful."

The old mouse with the mustache spoke up, then, throwing his head high and aloof, "In the old days, we made battle against The Toad King of the Sumbly Swamps to the north of Riverbank. Did these toads wear any telltale signs? What insignia did they wear on their shields and banners?" The mustachioed mouse looked up at Nova.

Juniper hung her head down, saying, "I don't recall seeing anything. Do you, Nova?"

"Yes, as a matter of fact," Nova the squirrel started, stroking her chin and squinting her eyes as if to recall, "I seem to remember that they had painted webbed toes on their shields, almost as if they had dipped their feet in paint and stamped it on there.

The old mouse with the mustache, who was the once well-renowned Captain Grubbels and veteran of the Great War of the Toads, nodded his head. "Aye, aye. That will be the mark of the Toads of the Sumbly Swamp and their King. Black are their flags and iron is their armor. Black are their capes, and I suspect their hearts are black as well. We have kept an eye on their movements, though we didn't want to bother any of the villagers with it. We didn't think they were dangerous. It seems we were wrong."

Father Holbrook, the elderly chipmunk, nodded his head and clasped his hands before him. "Nova, I believe fate has made a choice for you, today. You and your two friends, Juniper and Chordy, should go down to the kitchens and prepare a rucksack with provisions—at least a few days' worth. You shall scout ahead and track down the toads. Captain Grubbels, I am putting you in charge of raising a rescue party of two score hardy and healthy warriors who will follow behind Nova's party. I will see to the defenses at home and organize the arming of our warriors for the defense of Riverbank. These are grim and strange times, but we must rise to the occasion."

There were murmurs of agreement all throughout the gathering hall. Tankards and mugs of tea and porters and ales were clanked together, and some of the younger and eager villagers ran off right away to to the armory to fetch bows and slings and swords and armor.

The quiet hamlet of Riverbank was awakened from its sleepy slumber for the first time in years.

CHAPTER 4

Down in the Riverbank Village kitchens, there was a bustle of activity, as squirrels and mice and porcupines of all ages and sizes moved about, scrubbing pots and pans, baking cakes and fresh breads, peeling turnips and slicing purple carrots, and cutting wheels of aged, red cheddar cheese into wedges. The kitchens were normally quite busy, but now that preparations had already begun for the expedition to save Rudbeck from the toads, there was a well-ordered flurry of motion and commotion among the ovens and table-tops. Riverbank villagers loved to eat, and put great care and focus in the preparation of delicious meals and treat and drinks.

The head cook, the beloved gray squirrel Chef Kosta Goodknee, hobbled about the kitchens, barking orders in a playful, but boisterous manner in a baritone voice like a foghorn. He was called "Goodknee" because he had permanently injured his right knee as a child, and often said, "I still have one good knee, and I know how to use it!" when any of the kitchen staff got out of line. Though no one quite understood what the chef intended by the threat, they weren't too keen to find out what he meant.

Nevertheless, Chef Goodknee was widely loved by the villagers for his generosity in doling out enormous spoonfuls of his famous dishes, from heaping plates of summer salad with cranberry, walnut, and cheese crumbles to bottomless bowls of purple carrot stew in the long winters, or the chef's personal favorite: giant toasted sandwiches with honey, hot peppers, sweet peppers, red onion, and thickly sliced cheddar on fresh white nut bread, dressed with a secret oil that he made in the late night hours so none but him could know the recipe.

Chef Goodknee, a tall and heavy squirrel of healthy middle age and in the full swing of his prime years of life, was the undisputed master of the kitchens at Riverbank. He was also a great teller of tales and collector of songs and stories. As it was said in those days: "A good chef knows their way around a kitchen. But a great chef knows their audience." This was in fact a natural mutation of an even older proverb from the earliest days of Riverbank Village, when wise villagers liked to remark "Serve a salmon to a bear and a berry to a bird." One can easily imagine that this was a lesson learned rather painfully from practical experience.

"Hullo, my dear Nova," Chef Goodknee bellowed over the din and cacophony of the Riverbank kitchen. Flames were roaring and soups were bubbling and copper and iron pots were clanging and brushes were scrubbing all around them. "I've heard the news already, of course. You're to lead a tracking party while Captain Grubbels puts together an expeditionary force to follow. Father Holbrook will be organizing the wall guards and home defenses. Don't worry, I've got the menus all planned out. I've put together five days of rations for you and your two friends, there, and good fare, too, not too much of that hardtack and salted herring. No, you all deserve better than common soldiers' rations. This isn't some game we're playing," he twirled a shining chef's knife in the air and caught it in his paw, then slammed it down point first into the wooden table.

He continued with a grim look on his face, "No, this is no game. Riverbank is on the move, and I mean to feed our warriors with the best vittles we can muster. There's good, fresh nut bread in there, and plenty of almond butter, honey biscuits, toasted seed crackers, a flask of your favorite Valerian root tea, and, my new invention." Chef Goodknee held up a strange looking ball and smiled. "One of these will keep you good for a day or two, maybe more. No, our soldiers won't be eating weevily biscuits. Not on my watch. This is granola with cashew and walnut paste, dried blueberries, and dark, bitter chocolate chunks all rolled up into a perfect snack. Here, try one," and Chef Goodknee threw one of the unusual, chunky balls at Nova, who caught it nimbly.

She took a bite and offered some to Juniper and Chordy. "Hey, this is great! Try it!"

As they were munching on Chef Goodknee's curious and rather tasty invention, Nova sensed that a creature was looking at her from across the room. She thought she saw a red fox in a high-collared, blue and gray uniform exiting through a doorway just through the arch at the far side of the kitchens. But there was so much steam and commotion that she wasn't sure, so she shook her head and forgot about it.

Chef Goodknee gave Nova the red squirrel, Juniper the red rabbit, and Chordy the porcupine a rucksack filled with provisions for the road, and wished them good luck. The adventurers slung the packs over their backs. Chef Goodknee shook their paws and pulled a scrubbing brush down from a rack on the wall.

"Here, let me just fix your hairs for you," the chef said. "You lot should look the part before you set out on your journey. Never know what sort of a mess you'll be in by the time you return."

Juniper took one look at the dirty scrubbing brush with bits of egg and cheese and gray gunk stuck in the bristles, and said, "No thank you, Chef, that's quite alright. But thank you ever so much for the rations! We really must be going." And the three young adventurers hurried out of the kitchens with Chef Goodknee laughing to himself in his deep, warm, baritone voice.

The chef popped one of the granola, cashew, walnut, blueberry, and dark chocolate balls into his mouth and chewed on it with sincere pleasure. His right eyebrow shot up on the third bite. "Needs some rock salt, this does. Just a pinch. Yes, just a pinch."

CHAPTER 5

By the time the three young adventurers—Nova, Juniper, and Chordy—were ready to leave the village, the sun was high and the day was fully warmed. The blooms of spring decorated the gardens of Riverbank Village, and Nova felt a curious sense that it may be a while until she saw her home again, so she took one last look at her little stone home, the well-worn dirt pathways that winded through the village, the familiar trees and hanging lanterns, and the faces of the villagers she knew so well, before they went out of the gate of the village.

The battlements were now filled to the brim with eager recruits, who had donned a motley assortment of old armors and weapons from the Riverbank armory. They paced about the walls and kept a watch out into the Marchwood, keeping their eyes peeled for toads and strange tidings. High, billowing, white clouds like towers rose in the sky overhead, and every so often passed in front of the sun, casting a peaceful shade over the village and the greater woodlands.

As Nova led her friends through the gate and down the path back to the old spruce tree where Rudbeck was captured,

Captain Grubbels could be seen in the fields just before the tree line. Grubbels was waving his saber around and barking orders, his mustache bobbing and twitching as he tried to train and educate his troops on the arts of war—an art with which the peaceful inhabitants of Riverbank village were none too familiar. He had selected a group of warriors to form the expeditionary force in the rescue of Rudbeck, though they did not look entirely too prepared for the task. It had been a long time since Riverbank had to muster its arms for battle.

As they passed, Grubbels looked over to the path and shouted after them, "Steady on! We'll follow in an hour's time! I need to get these recruits in shape. They'll be ready, don't you worry!"

Nova took a deep breath and relaxed her shoulders as she walked onward. The afternoon light and breeze were swelling to just the right temperature, and she felt a sense of calm serenity under the ancient and peaceful trees of the forest. Even if the circumstances were somewhat grim, it was an excellent day to be out in the Marchwood.

"I worry about poor Rudbeck, of course, but I think he will be alright. We'll rescue him. And then we'll have a great feast back at the village. Won't that be nice? I'd love some of Chef Goodknee's creamy tomato soup tonight, with fresh golden nut bread with a big pad of salted butter right on top." Nova licked her lips at the thought.

Chordy nodded his head. He was using the staff of his poleaxe as one might use a walking stick. "That would do the trick. But I can hardly think of eating at the moment. I'm just excited to be out on the trails and on my very own quest. This is just what I needed, you know. I've been up on those walls for years dreaming of a real adventure. Captain Grubbels said the Toad King lives in a castle to the north. Do you think that's where they've taken Rudbeck?"

"I believe that was the plan, though we should keep an eye out for anything suspicious. We're in charge of tracking. So we'll go to the old spruce and see if there's any sign of which way they went."

The young adventurers fell right into their roles. Everything seemed bright and full of opportunity at that moment. Even the dry dust of the dirt path seemed to glitter in the sunlight, as they listened to the soundscape of robins, finches, and warblers mixing together with the whistling of the great crested flycatcher and the squeaking of the yellow-bellied sapsucker. Off in the distance they heard the *chap-chap-chap-chap* of the marsh wren, clacking its beak like two stones clicking together.

The Marchwoods were alive and glowing with the spring, as vines began to climb up trees and between stones, and honey bees visited the wildflowers and young dragonflies moved about in the brush, settling on the fresh leaves of saplings. Last autumn's fallen leaves covered parts of the path and slowly returned to the ground to be taken back by the soil. The thick layer of old leaves smelled wet and wormy and worldly, in a sweet and pleasant way, and made cover and food for every manner of beetle and ant and friendly bug under their paws.

When one is in the woods, on a day like this, one feels altogether connected again to the very fabric of the world. The green, calming canopy of branches and leaves overhead lets sunlight trickle through from above in just the right dose, and the breeze is filtered through miles and miles of trees and bush and carries the scent of every flowering dogwood and every freshwater spring and pond, mingling with every lake and river and stream and every good creature that walks through the halls of the forest. In the woods, one senses there is no evil, no greed, no tyrant, no oppressor, no malady, but indeed a deep wellspring of *meaning* returns. To be connected to the woods is to be connected to the very art of life itself, and to walk along the stones and mosses, and under the tall trees and over the fallen trees and alongside the wet, rotten stumps is to be reminded of the great circus mystery and magic of being itself.

Such was the place where Nova's thoughts began to wander relaxedly as she looked out into the very far horizon of the trees, into the place where individual trees become a forest, and you can almost see the precise place where one tree becomes many trees and many trunks simply become "the woods," and all the eye can see extends onward into a dark green fabric into the distance, seemingly forever.

But Chordy, at that moment, broke into a walking song and nearly startled Nova and Juniper:

My paws are on the trails in the merry months of spring
From hill to valley low and mountain high

I thank the roots and trees and the cherries that will bring
A nice surprise when baked inside a pie!

The winding trails of life will carry me along
There's seldom sorrow sitting in my heart
For I just simply sing our merry little song
For never are my love and I apart!

For my love is in the woods, in the berries and the branch
And I can always visit when I like
I just walk along the trails, as I've always got the chance
To wander off and take a little hike!

Nova and Juniper joined in with Chordy, and it wasn't long before they were inventing new verses to the old walking song and laughing and having a good time together. Juniper managed to scoop up a handful of early spring blackberries and tossed them to her friends. When they reached the old spruce tree with the hollow in it, where Rudbeck had been captured by the toads, they sat down on a fallen tree and started to dig into their packs for some lunch.

"Did you hear something just now?" Nova asked, digging around in her rucksack.

There was a loud *seebit-seebit-seebit* followed by a trill.

"Sounds like a warbler, maybe. Though I couldn't tell you which kind. I learned all about warblers from my cousins, growing up down by the riverbank on the River Reed. You know I grew up by the old water wheel and the mill, right? Well, my cousins loved birds and told me all about them. There's every sort of warbler you could think of. There's the cape warbler, the blue warbler, the black-throated blue warbler, the northern warbler, and the black and white warbler, just to start. Then you've got the black-throated green warbler, the chestnut-sided warbler..."

Nova smiled at her friend, appreciating her thoroughness and attention to detail. "No, it wasn't a bird. I thought I heard something in the grass rustling around. Could it be Captain Grubbels and his troops catching up with us already? I'm afraid we haven't made much progress to speak of. Poor Rudbeck..."

But Nova's ears had not deceived her, for a sneaky red fox in a dusty, blue and gray uniform with a high collar just then

44

appeared from out of the bushes, brandishing a broad sword with intricate carvings and runes carved into the shining, polished blade. His eyes glimmered a bright, oceanic blue, and he approached with his sword drawn!

CHAPTER 6

The red fox did not say anything, but stared at the companions, bouncing his sword from paw to paw and back again.

Nova, Juniper, and Chordy braced for action. They steadied their footpaws and drew their weapons. Nova unsheathed the short sword from her back, while Chordy gripped his poleaxe with bow paws and made a frightening grimace with his teeth bared. Juniper twirled a hardwood staff that she had grabbed from the armory before they left, having studied some of the ancient martial arts with the chipmunks in her earlier years when she was just a young leveret growing up on the banks of the River Reed.

"Whoah, hold on, there!" the red fox stammered, lowering his sword. "I've come from Riverbank. I want to help you."

They all breathed a sigh of relief and put their weapons down.

"You sure gave us quite a freight. What are you doing sneaking around and following us? We could have mistaken you for an enemy. These are strange times in Marchwood..."

Nova was not truly angry, but she was a bit flustered at the surprise.

"What's your name," Chordy asked. "And what's your business?"

"You can call me Foxy. I'm new to the village, so maybe you haven't seen me around much. I just came here from the Eastern Woods. There's trouble brewing in those parts. So I've come to start a new life."

"Come, sit with us and we'll share some of our rations. We may as well have a lunch together and make a good time of it. Won't we, now?" Nova offered her paw to the young red fox in the well-worn and dirty uniform. He came and sat on the log with the adventurers, who dug right into eating their lunch. Foxy's hair was scruffy and mussy, and he had a bit of a wild scent to him.

"I was in the gathering hall when Father Holbrook was speaking. I figured you might need help with your tracking. I'm an expert scout and tracker! I trained as a ranger growing up not far from Goldengrove."

"Do you miss your home? What's Goldengrove like?" Juniper asked.

"I do miss it. But it's nice, here," Foxy remarked, looking up at the tall trees. "Goldengrove is a lot bigger. There are fewer trees in those parts. And everyone's always running around with business. Life seems slower, here. And I like that. But still, the footpaws get restless after a while. Do you know what I mean?" He grinned a toothsome grin and happily snacked on a pawful of crackers that they shared with him. He talked with a mouthful of crackers and spat crumbs as he talked. "My father always said, 'Foxy, you should live somewhere where there are more trees than people. It tells you something about the place. If the folks value trees more than business, then you're in good company.' Or something like that. I'm sure it was more eloquent than that. He was a real talker."

Nova looked up at the sky. She could see some clouds through the tops of the trees, as there was a bit of a clearing near the old spruce with the hollow in it. She hadn't seen her father in ages, and wondered where he was at that moment.

"Do you miss your father, Foxy? You talk of him as in the past. I haven't seen my father in a long time, either."

A strange light perked up in the red fox's swirly, blue, marble-like eyes, and he sighed. "I'm sure we'll have plenty of time to talk about that. No matter. It's a great day for ranging through the woods. I tell you what," he grabbed another handful of crackers and stuffed them in his mouth, crunching loudly as he talked. "I tell you what, I already picked up on the trail of the toads. They've cut straight north through the woods, right to the castle of the Toad King. I've been up that way, before. It's a bit of a journey, but we'll make it by this very evening if we get on with things."

The friends were shocked, and Chordy puffed out his chest, asking "You've seen the Sumbly Swamps and the castle of the Toad King? Whatever were you doing that way? Isn't it dangerous?"

"Not too dangerous, if you know your way around. I get bored around the village, so I go exploring and see what trouble... err, see what I can find. You find lots of things in the woods. Like this sword." He picked up his blade and rocked it back and forth in his paw, letting the light shine and shimmer off the polished steel. "It's a curious blade. It fits my paw like it was made for it. I found it in a cave just westerly from the village. I can't quite recall the place, lots of big trees and strange lights in the waters. Fireflies all over. Big orange flowers. Seemed almost magical."

They had heard tales of the Firelily Grove, where fireflies congregated and giant orange flowers towered overhead, but none of them had ever laid eyes upon it.

"Well, Foxy, it seems like we'll have a great deal to talk about, no doubt about it. And now our lunch is over. Come on, everyone, we have to save Rudbeck!" Nova jumped off the log and slung her pack and shortsword around her shoulder, and felt the weight of it bounce off her back. "Or, that is, if you wouldn't mind leading the way, Foxy. Would you mind?"

"No problem at all, that's why I'm here!" Foxy grinned his toothsome grin and swung his arms gladly. He was happy to be among good company and new friends, and was eager to get the adventure underway.

CHAPTER 7

As the party of four went further onward to the north, they slowly noticed, almost imperceptibly, that the forest was changing. The land around Riverbank felt different under their paws, getting damp and marshy and mossy. Red maple, silver maple, and green ash grew everywhere, and ferns sprung up green and spindly all around them. New red maple saplings with smooth bark crowded the edges of the path, and the path itself became more winding and hillier as it went up and down, with broad puddles that they needed to jump over. Hummocks, old stumps, and large logs were scattered about, sometimes having fallen over the path itself. Marsh marigolds and cardinal flower made rich understories all about the trees.

The birdsong grew louder, too, as they watched all manner of birds flying about overhead, eating overripe winterberry and spicebush. Fresh viburnum fruit was red and rich and hung from the branches overhead and off to their left and right.

"We're certainly not in Riverbank anymore," Chordy chuckled. "This is a wild country. Beautiful, though."

"These are marshlands," Foxy noted. "You have to watch for flooding in the spring. The mountain melts can flood the rivers."

"What, the high mountains? But they're so far away." Juniper was puzzled.

"It's all connected, you know. The snow melts in the spring on the high mountains, and it comes down in torrents and waterfalls and *whoosh,*" Foxy made a sweeping motion with his paws, "it *whooshes* right from the high peaks into the riverlands, and floods the rivers, which flood the marshes, and from the rivers it goes to the lakelands to the south, and no one knows where it goes after that. Maybe back to the sky or to other rivers and lakes. The chipmunks in Riverbank say it all flows to the Great River. The same Great River where we all go, in the end."

Chordy chuckled, "I wouldn't mind taking a boat down the Great River. It must go somewhere."

Foxy nodded, "There are maps and scholars in Goldengrove who are working on the charting. They ought to speak to the chipmunks, here. I think they would have knowledge to share with each other. There's bound to be truth, somewhere between the methods. It's always like that."

Nova was impressed with Foxy's learning and academic musings. And even if she didn't agree with everything he was saying, she enjoyed listening to the new words and ideas that he was sharing. It was good to get a fresh perspective. There weren't often fresh perspectives, growing up in the sleepy village of Riverbank, which is why she turned to books and scrolls in her youth.

"Hold up!" Foxy yipped. "There's something here, on the path."

Juniper knelt down next to Nova and Foxy. There, where the path had turned quite muddy, they saw the webbed footprints of many toads, who looked to be in a great hurry, judging by the deep impressions they made into the mud, which was now hardening and baking in the hot afternoon sun. Set inside one of the webbed footprints on the path was a copper pinecone with a chain attached to it.

"That's Rudbeck's charm!" Nova recognized the necklace right away.

"He must have dropped it to leave a trail for you," Foxy remarked. "Smart fellow, this Rudbeck. I'll look forward to meeting him. He wanted you to find it."

The day went on, and the party of four made their way through the marshlands of Marchwood, continuing on the winding path. Foxy knew the way, and directed them first left, then right after two forks in the path. "This one leads back around toward Riverbank," he mused. "You don't want to take the wrong path, or we'll turn a day's journey into five days. There's one up ahead that stretches all the way to the High Road and goes on to the canyon lands, if you follow it all the way."

Juniper nodded her head. She never considered how far the paths of the woods might lead or where they might go. "I suppose the paths are all connected, too," she thought, "like the rivers and the waters."

The afternoon turned to evening and the crew stopped again for a brief break. They found a big, sturdy, gray and black stone to sit on, with a nice, flat top. They took the fresh nut bread out of their packs, and made simple, tidy sandwiches with almond butter spread, and sipped strong Valerian tea with lemongrass from the flasks that Chef Goodknee had provided for them. Foxy foraged some apples from a spot nearby he remembered, and shared them with Nova, Juniper, and Chordy. In turn, the three shared their provisions with Foxy. They didn't stop for long, and kept munching away as they continued walking.

Afternoon turned to evening, and evening to dusk. The birdsong changed and the color of the sky above morphed from the whites and blues of daytime to the purples and royals of the night. It grew dark earlier in the woods than in the clearings, as less light filters through the heavily wooded marshes, and their eyes were slow to adjust. They were not accustomed to being out in the woods at night, as they usually made small fires in fireplaces and lit candles in their homes and spent the evenings in cozy comfort, as most Riverbank Villagers were keen to do.

"Will we reach the Toad King's castle by nightfall, Foxy? I hadn't much thought of what we're going to do when we get there. And what about Captain Grubbels? Do you think the Riverbank soldiers are far behind? What if we come across some wild toads on the road? Is the path guarded?" Juniper was growing worried as they went further and further into the woods.

"It's alright, I know what I'm doing," Foxy reassured her. "I've been this way before. The path to the castle is seldom used, and the toads always go inside at night. They hole up in the castle and shut the front gate most of the time. Some patrols go in and out during the day. As to what your plan is, I have no idea. I just came along to help. I'm not much of a strategist, frankly," Foxy threw the green, crisp apple he was carrying in his paw up into the air, and caught it again, spinning it around. Then he took a big, crunching bite into the semi-sour fruit.

Chordy joined in, "Maybe the cover of night will give us an advantage. Do you think we could sneak in and save Rudbeck?"

The company of four continued to discuss their plan and weigh their options. Foxy led them off the path and over a hill. The ground was wet and swampy and muddy, and they had to be careful their footpaws didn't get stuck in the slopping mud. Little flies and mosquitoes made clouds overhead and landed in their fur, and buzzed in their ears. They swatted them away as best as they could.

Foxy unfurled a bundle of herbs from the pocket of his tattered old uniform, and distributed them to the group. It was an ancient herbal repellent that his father had taught him, made from peppermint, lemon balm, and basil, rolled together.

"It's important to rub it together really well, so that you release the oils from the leaves," he said. He rubbed it all over his head. "Doesn't smell too bad, either." He took a deep whiff. Nova and the others did the same, and the repellent helped to keep the bugs away for a time. Chordy rubbed a little under his nose, liking the scent overmuch.

They marched on and rose over the crest of a hill. Nova and Juniper nearly gasped with amazement, as they saw the black stone towers of the Toad King's castle rising high into the sky, just over the hill. Cattails and swampgrass grew heavily all around the castle. In the growing dark of the dusk, the three tall black towers of the castle rose high overhead, with sharp spires like needles dotting the rooftops. A large, dark iron and wood gate was fastened shut. They noticed there weren't many windows, but statues of big toads with tridents sat like gargoyles watching from the battlements. In the dying daylight, they thought it looked ominous, though Nova wasn't sure if it was just an illusion of the light.

While toads are great engineers, the castle had not been built by their kind. It was raised long ago by the ingenious pine martens who once lived in those parts. With the changing of the ages, the once fertile and forested gully had become marshier, and better suited to the toads, who took residence in the then-abandoned castle. Some say the pine martens cut too much of the timber and changed the land for the worse, though others thought the martens had done their best to replant the trees they took, and that the land was changing of its own accord. In the present day, as the friends looked on, it did not appear well-kept.

"Fancy us, sneaking into that place. It looks rough as can be," Nova muttered. "I wonder if there's another way in. That gate isn't going to budge for the likes of us." The front gate indeed looked impenetrable.

Foxy nodded. "Three steps ahead of you, Nova. There's a small backdoor, and the cooks empty out their waste after the evening feasts. We've just made it in time. We'll miss Captain

Grubbels, unless he shows up soon, but I suspect the Riverbank warriors can fend for themselves. If we hurry we can make it in time and get through the back door and then look for Rudbeck. The trouble is, once we're inside, we'll have to be careful as can be. We can get *in* easy enough, but it will be a lot harder to get *out*."

Nova nodded. "In Riverbank, the elders always fall asleep after a big meal. I suppose toads might do the same. If there's a good time to break in there, it's going to be now, after their feasting."

They all looked at each other and nodded. The plan was set!

CHAPTER 8

Foxy, the young red fox in the high-collared, foreign uniform, led Nova, Juniper, and Chordy around the edge of the woods near the castle. The hills and treeline were very close to the castle, so they were able to sneak about in the woods undetected without much trouble. They crept along in the brush, walking bent over and with quiet pawsteps. They grew nervous as they drew closer. They circled around the enormity of the black castle of the toad king until they came around the back. From there, they snuck up behind some bushes that had grown close to the backdoor.

It seemed everywhere to be overgrown and untended. Toads are not known for their cultivation of gardens, though they can be honest farmers. Their thumbs are often green, after all.

The plan, as they had decided, was to wait for the toad cooks in the castle to open the back door and empty out their waste from the toad's meal. What the friends did not know, however, was that dinnertime at Riverbank was equivalent to breakfast in the black castle, as these were nocturnal toads who kept different hours—the toads were just beginning their day's work and would be on the alert. As the friends hid, waiting, they noticed an unwholesome smell of burned bread, gray meat, rotting peels, sour milks, and old eggs all around them.

"I suspect we're not too far away from where they take out the trash. It stinks around here." Juniper plugged her nose.

"*Hush.* Here, put a little of this up your nose." Foxy handed them some of the peppermint herb that was rolled up in his pocket. "But be quiet. We don't want to be seen. That would be trouble for all of us. Once we're inside, we need to stick together, and let's not get lost. It's a big castle. We'll search the basements for Rudbeck. Prisons are usually in the basements of these old castles."

Everyone nodded. Nova adjusted the green wool cap on her head. The way it fit just right on her head renewed her confidence. She felt her favorite handkerchief in her pocket, with the blue paisley pattern. It comforted her.

They could just start to hear the nighttime songsters of the woods starting to let their melodies fly out over the open airs. Loons, barred owls, and sandpipers let their songs be heard over the marshlands. From the direction of the castle, they heard the commotion of the kitchen in full swing, and from a window high above, they heard the sounds of bass drums and rhythmic chanting, and high pitched bone flutes. There was the clanking of mugs and hot, red firelight glowed from the windows.

The four sat behind the bushes, sitting low to the ground, listening and waiting. Nova felt a nervousness rising up in her, and Juniper trembled slightly. Most nights, they would be seated in front of a cozy fire with a book or an instrument, or feasting with friends, or dancing in the gathering hall under the Meadow Tower to the sounds of the hurdy-gurdy and the woodland kithara. But now, they were poised on the very edge of danger itself, and Nova doubted herself.

But there was no time for doubt. They all four heard the creak of the backdoor of the castle open, and out came a very large toad wearing a greasy, stained apron and a crooked hat. The toad was sweating profusely, and in both of his webbed hands he carried a metal bucket of stinking slop. He kicked a doorstop underneath the door, so it remained open just half a foot. The toad was muttering to himself under his breath, and through the bush, they watched him walk down a light trail, barely visible in the growing darkness, still talking to himself, complaining of his duties.

"Now's our chance. Let's go! Their waste pile is just down the bend over there. He'll be back soon."

They dashed to the door, and burst into the kitchens of the castle of the Toad King! Unfortunately, everything went wrong. Everything went wrong immediately.

There were, of course, at least a dozen toads still working in the kitchens, and they all let out a collective croak of surprise to see these intruders burst through the door. Chordy took no chances, and immediately let loose with his massive poleaxe, and swept away the two toads closest to him, who were sent tumbling into a pushcart that was piled high with dirty dishes and mugs and decanters that went cracking and splattering all over the stone floor of the kitchen.

Foxy leapt up onto the center table and bared his teeth, grimacing and growling, and letting out a mad yip as he struck out with his blade. He slashed and hacked with his broad sword, knocking the ladle from a toad's hand. But another toad, thinking fast, had grabbed a great butcher's cleaver and sliced down at Foxy's foot. Foxy just moved his toes in time, and bashed the toad on the top of his head with the broadside of his blade, knocking him over.

Most of the toads scattered, but three burly looking ones stood their ground. They were all wearing aprons. One brandished the butcher's cleaver he picked up from the table, one carried a massive cast iron pan, and the last held a dirty, wicked looking mop.

The toad with the iron pan dashed forward at Juniper, who struck back with her hardwood staff. The toad raised the cast iron pan in front of his face just in time to block the attack, and a deafening *clang!* rang out and echoed throughout the kitchen, and her hands were fairly numbed from the vibrations that traveled up her staff. Nova jumped in to the rescue, and used her short sword to knock the pan from the toad's hands. She pushed him out of the way, and faced down the toad cooks with the butcher's cleaver and the mop, standing side by side.

The toad with the mop stepped forward, twirling the mop in a dizzying circle in front of him.

Nova stabbed with her short sword, but the toad was incredibly nimble and adept with the mop, surprising them all with his acrobatics. He hopped—as toads are great jumpers and very quick on their toes—up onto the center table, and kicked a steaming pan of tepid larvae stew into Nova's face, and she sputtered and coughed and jumped back. Chordy blasted forward with his massive frame, and shook his quills in anger. He swung out with the poleaxe, but the toad with the mop deftly met the blow and nearly knocked the poleaxe from Chordy's hands.

They were well matched fighters, and the battle would have ensued much longer, but the toads threw down their weapons and hopped out of the hall.

"I bet they're off to get reinforcements! Let's get out of here," Juniper yelled, and the others followed.

CHAPTER 9

Nova the red squirrel took the lead, and Foxy the fox, Juniper the rabbit, and Chordy the porcupine followed behind them as they quietly walked through the halls of the black castle of the Toad King.

"We won't have a lot of time," Nova whispered, though everything she said sounded loud as it reverberated and echoed in the empty stone hallways. Mismatched sconces with old, ugly candles hung from the ceiling in seemingly random locations, giving off dull, orange and yellow light in the dark, winding passageways. They could hear their own footpads making a dull *thomp* as they walked along the stone floors. Somewhere, they heard a dripping sound.

"We need to go down," Foxy said. "They always keep prisoners in the basement, in the dungeons, you know? That's how these old castles always work. There are castles near Goldengrove," he started to say, but then stopped himself. "Well, it's a long story. Let's see if we can find some stairs that lead into the basements."

The notion was disquieting to the party, but it was now too late to leave. They were determined to find their friend, Rudbeck the mouse, and unchain him from the captivity of the Toad King.

The twisting and winding halls of the old castle seemed like a labyrinth to the young adventurers. But they did not despair, for they knew they must act quickly, and they soon found an archway that led into a spacious, carpeted library with couches and benches and a large fireplace. Shelves of disorganized books and glass bottles and jars lined every wall. A single toad was sitting in a wide, comfortable, red chair, smoking a pipe and crunching on something black and sticky. He looked thoroughly preoccupied, and had his feet propped up on a stool. The toad blew little smoke rings and hummed a bit of an old marching tune as he snacked. A great roaring fire was going in the hearth at the head of the room, over which was hung a painting of the castle in its better days. It was a cozy nook in the otherwise damp basement of the castle.

"You know, maybe this place isn't so bad," Chordy muttered under his breath. "I like the looks of this library. I could spend a few hours in here. And look, there, on the table. I'll bet you those are the keys to the dungeon cells."

The toad—who they imagined was a guard—sat facing away from them, toward the hearth and the fire. To his right was a stone end table, on which was placed a large mug and a giant key ring with scores of iron skeleton keys.

Chordy started tip-toeing over to the chair and shook his head, wondering at his own audacity. He came up behind the toad smoking the pipe, and put his paws over the toads mouth, who let out a muffled squeal. The pipe fell out of his mouth and the tobacco spilled onto his lap. "Don't say a word and I'll let ya' live," Chordy muttered. "We just want the keys to the cell."

"Mrrrrrf-mhmmm-rmmmmph! Ermmmmph-phrummmm-frmmm!" The toad looked at them and tried to talk but Chordy's big paws covered and muffled his mouth.

"Don't say a word, and don't call for help. Do you understand?" Chordy threatened in a whisper.

The toad nodded.

"I want you to lead us down to the dungeons."

The toad nodded again, slowly.

Chordy took his hands off the toad's mouth, and he hopped out of his seat. He was wearing a long evening robe of a thick, dark brown fabric. The toad picked up his pipe and stuffed the tobacco back into it, put his webbed feet into his slippers, and pointed toward the archway to his left.

Through the archway was a straight and narrow stone staircase that went down, down, down, and deeper down. At the bottom of the staircase, the toad in the robe turned around and pointed to the key ring in Chordy's hands. Chordy handed them over.

"No funny business, now, Mr. Toad. We don't mean any harm. We're just here to rescue our friend Rudbeck. For your sake, I hope he's still alive down here."

The toad shrugged his shoulders, opened the iron door to the dungeons, and held the door open for the intruders.

They all shouted in unison, "Rudbeck? Rudbeck!" and "Where are you, Rudbeck?" The dungeons were cold and damp and drippy, and the stone floor was mossy and slippery. There seemed to be water coming in through cracks in the foundation of the castle, and there was a musty, sickly smell throughout.

But the dungeon cells were all completely *empty*.

Juniper ran down the length of the long hall, looking in every cell. The iron doors were all open, and not a single prisoner was to be seen in the dungeon. Every cell was entirely unoccupied and fully cleaned out, as if they hadn't been used in years.

"There's no one here," Juniper yelled out to her friends, when she had reached the end of the hallway. Nova was right behind her.

Foxy turned around and grabbed the guard toad by his robe, and pulled him close to his face. "What kind of trick is this, toady? Where's our friend? What did you do with the mouse you captured?"

Nova and Juniper ran back from the end of the hallway.

The toad gurgled and croaked but then Foxy let him go and his voice cleared. "I tried to tell you, but the massive paws of your esteemed companion, here, interrupted my explanation." The toad seemed to be surprisingly well-mannered and civil. "We keep no prisoners in our dungeon, not for an entire generation. I think you've misinterpreted something." The toad grinned at them.

"Then where's our friend? You've executed him? How could you?" Nova cried out.

The stomping of heavy boots and clanking armor and spears echoed throughout the air as a swarm of guards made their way down the long length of narrow stairs into the dungeon.

"There's no way out," Foxy sighed. "We're trapped in a dead end. Sorry, friends."

They were all of a sudden surrounded by the guards of the Toad King, brandishing their spears. The guards wearing battle-worn armors and plates with spears and shields vastly outnumbered the four companions. They hardly had time to surrender their arms before they were swept up by the Toad King's armed guards and were dragged, kicking and biting and yelling all the way up the stairs to the main throne room of the Toad King.

CHAPTER 10

In the halls of the Toad King, long tables were laid out with giant beeswax candles that looked like great globs and blobs. Dishes and cups and mugs were scattered everywhere, and platters and plates were stacked with the fare of the evening feast of the toads in the black castle.

There were puddings and jams with beetle bread, barrels of a mealy, thick brew that smelled of corn and acid, and heaps of crunchy, black shells littered about. A band of toads played on their instruments from a corner, with a small accordion, bone whistles, and drums. Bowls of overripe tomatoes and giant white onions sat in the middle of every table. Nothing so pleased a toad in those days as a bite of a fresh, raw, white onion to cleanse the palate between bites of a hearty meal.

The Toad King sat on his high, black throne at a table set on the dais, with the captains of his guard sitting on either side of him, deep into their meal and their cups of oat brew. He struck an imposing figure in his aged, dented armor, and cracked, bent crown. Though the crown was old and in poor repair, it was high and huge on the Toad King's head, and looked sinister with its thin needle-like points and dark, black gems set into the rusting metal. One of his eyes was a bloody, crimson red, and one was black as night. In truth, he was suffering from a mild insomnia and had been rubbing at a sore stye in his right eye—an infection that had been painful and bothersome.

As the armored toad guards of the Toad King hauled the four friends through the gathering hall, scores of toads stood up from their seats, straightened their hats, dusted crumbs off their tunics and uniforms, and blinked their eyes in surprise. It had been an unusual day in the black castle of Sumbly Swamp. They watched as the guards dragged the kicking and grumbling prisoners through the hall and toward the dais.

"Let go of these prisoners. *Briiiibit.* That's no way to handle guests in our halls," the Toad King bellowed out. His voice was round and mellow, and reverberated smoothly through the high-ceilings of the great hall, much to the company's surprise. They imagined he would yell at them horribly in a sinister manner, but it was pleasant to listen to his royal speech, which was occasionally interrupted by a delicate croak like a hiccup: *briiibit, briiibit.*

The guards let go of the prisoners and they stumbled, brushing themselves off and standing up straight, looking up the stairs to the dais. Then, they recognized the face of Rudbeck seated up at the Toad King's long table on the dais, in a seat of honor!

"Rudbeck! What are you doing up there?" Nova called out in shock. It wasn't polite to speak out of turn in the presence of the Toad King, but it didn't occur to her at that moment. She was shocked to see their captured friend sitting next to the toads.

Rudbeck had a contented look on his face, and his belly was full, and crumbs were scattered all over his cloak. A bit of toadish grog was on his chin. Rudbeck the mouse looked quite full and happy, indeed, and certainly safe and sound. He waved at his friends.

The Toad King spoke again. "I gather you've come looking for your friend. You've caused quite a stir in our kitchens, though, and that won't do, *briiibit,*" the Toad King called out. He bore a serious expression, then, but his face turned jovial as he started to laugh. "You gave our cooks quite the freight! I hear there was an incident with a broom."

Nova, Juniper, Chordy, and Foxy were silent. They looked up to the Toad King, and then to Rudbeck, wondering all the while what events had unfolded before they arrived.

"But I do owe you an explanation and an apology. Rudbeck, here, is our honored guest, today. You see, there has been ill news on the wind, and we needed a villager of Riverbank to report to us the going-ons of the wars in the East. Unfortunately, he has done more eating than reporting. He knows very little. In fact I believe we have much more to share with you than you have to share with us. Your tiny village of Riverbank has been cut off from the wider Marchwood for far too long, *briiiibit.*" The Toad King leaned back in his throne and took a swig from a hand-carved, black stone stein. He burped politely and gave out another croak.

"What about the necklace? The pinecone amulet? We thought you left a trail for us to follow to save you," Juniper wondered aloud.

"Oh, you found my pinecone charm! I must have dropped it while we were traveling. I suppose the toads did technically capture me, but they've been great hosts," Rudbeck answered.

The young adventurers were too perplexed for words, and approached the Toad King's high table. He stood and pulled chairs out for his guests. The captains of his guard moved down the table to make room for the visitors. They all sat down at the table. Drinks were passed down to them and mugs were filled with the thick oat brew.

"I don't understand. What ill news do you speak of, Toad King? We've heard of war in the East from our new friend, Foxy. But there's been no ill winds that we know of, nothing that I've heard..." Nova was a bit shaken from the battle in the kitchens and was still trying to make sense of the situation. She had thought that she would be imprisoned or worse in the dungeons of the Toad King.

"Marchwood is at war, my dear. You have much bigger fish to fry than your immediate neighbors in the Sumbly Swamps. We mean no harm to you. You've misjudged us, unfortunately. Ah! *Briiibit.* Here are our other guests. An old friend of mine, Captain Grubbels." The Toad King pronounced this name with some apparent irritation.

The large, armored toads standing guard at the main entrance to the hall flung open the double doors, and into the

Toad King's hall marched Captain Grubbels, the mustachioed mouse, leading two score of Riverbank warriors, armed to the teeth.

CHAPTER 11

"Welcome, my old friend," the Toad King croaked sonorously, his voice bouncing around the high ceilings and black stone walls of the castle.

Captain Grubbels of Riverbank Village stepped proudly toward the throne on the dais with a stern expression on his face, leading two score of heavily armed and armored Riverbank Village warriors who had set out on the trails earlier that day. They were not an impressive bunch, as many were slumped over from the day's tiring and fast-paced march, and most were dust-covered and worn. The Riverbank villagers were not yet seasoned warriors.

Nova noticed that the toads were not alarmed by the influx of armed warriors into their halls. Then Foxy nudged her, and pointed up to the mezzanine. On both sides of the hall, there were archers, tall toads with iron bows, with full quivers of arrows at the ready.

The Toad King stood up, and his crown wobbled on his head. "My old friend, I do hope you come in peace into my halls. You see I welcome you with open arms and tables laid. Come and feast with us."

Grubbels stopped fifteen feet from the dais, at the head of his forces. "We won't dine with the likes of you. I know your kind. I was there, fifty years ago!" Grubbels nearly lost his temper and his voice rose, but he controlled himself, and continued. "You know what happened to the toad kings of old when they tried to meddle in our affairs. Riverbank is a peaceful village, and we've come to claim your prisoner, our friend Rudbeck." He drew his saber. "You give us Rudbeck, and we'll leave your halls in peace," he glared at the Toad King. "But if you dont," he said, as his voice lowered to a growl, "then there'll be a price to pay."

The Toad King let out a creaking, croaking chuckle and clasped his hands over his belly.

"You're in no position to make threats, my friend. Besides, we have *much* to talk about. Look, here." The Toad King gestured to Rudbeck. "Your 'prisoner' is well fed and cared for. He is our guest, today. Here is what you do not understand. We are a peaceful colony and mean you no harm," the king sighed. "It has been decades of misunderstanding between us.

And you have misjudged not only my people," he waved his arms, gesturing over the heads of the toads of his halls, "but you have misjudged the world around you. For many years my people have defended these lands from the great rhino beetles who would have overrun your tiny hamlet. We have hunted and consumed the locusts who would have devoured your gardens and ravaged your orchards. While you have grown old and stout, we have made possible the sleepy peace of your village. Yet you give us no thanks, and treat us even now as enemies. If I were more hasty, I would label this a malevolent prejudice against our kind. *Briiiibit.*"

Nova sat at the edge of her seat and gripped the armrests on her chair at the table. She couldn't discern whether the Toad King was merely a persuasive speaker, or whether he was truthful. She waited in anticipation to hear what Grubbels would say, but he did not speak. There was a tense silence.

The sturdy and veteran mouse, Captain Grubbels, sheathed his saber, and plucked at his mustache anxiously.

"But you are not too hasty. Go on," was all Grubbels said. "Go on with it, then. What do you want?"

The Toad King waved his arms, gesturing dramatically. "There is ill news on the wind. Alumbrial the Grave has raised a wretched army that sweeps through the towns of the East and now makes for the city of Goldengrove. Marchwood is at war while you warm your feet by your fires and pick your berries. This is why we have taken Rudbeck, for questioning. For you would not meet with us openly."

Foxy looked white as a sheet, as if the news stirred him especially.

Grubbels nodded his head. "There was the incident last month with the toads by our village, but... we thought they were spies."

"Indeed, they were not! We have tried many times to make contact with you, to form an alliance. A treaty! Do you know," the Toad King lowered his voice to nearly a whispering croak, "they say there is a great gray wolf who has come down from the mountains of the Far North, waving banners and rallying bands of rogues to his call, and his forces have swelled to the thousands? Riverbank Village would be overrun in not hours, but minutes, from either of these threats: Alumbrial in the

81

East and the great gray wolf in the North. There is more to the Marchwood than bread and ale, my dear Grubbels."

There was a loud murmur that went up from the Riverbank Village forces, still standing in the middle of the gathering hall. The toad archers with the iron bows in the mezzanine relaxed their aim, as the Toad King signaled to them with a lowering of his webbed hand, and waited for the tense meeting to unfold.

"There is truth in your words, Krub, King of Toads," Grubbels admitted, sighing. "And I am old, and my soldiers are weary. We mean no harm to you. I can see our good friend Rudbeck looks fine as can be. What does this young one say? Have you been harmed, Rudbeck?"

The mouse was roused from his sleepy state at the mention of his name. He had been feasting in the company of the toads for hours and hours, and his eyelids were getting heavy.

"Well, it's been an interesting couple of days for me, for sure! You see, I got stuck up in the hollow of this old spruce tree when I was climbing some mushrooms. At first I was looking at the fungus, I swore I saw one moving. Then I considered the medicinal properties of the mushroom, but I didn't have my field guide with me, so I just took a sample to examine later. Then I noticed the old hollow in the tree and figured I should go look up there," the mouse scratched his head as he went through his memories. "Then the mushroom shelf under my feet broke off, and I got stuck. There wasn't much in there, just an old nest and oh, an old note with some writing that I couldn't read. I think I gave that note to Nova. You know, and then the toads captured me, but they've been great hosts," Rudbeck turned to his left and right and smiled at his new friends. "Great dinner! Thank you all for your hospitality. Turns out they just wanted to chatter a bit. Too bad I don't keep my ear to the ground much, though. There wasn't anything I could tell them of interest," Rudbeck sat back in his padded chair at the dais and started picking his teeth nonchalantly.

Nova the red squirrel stood up. "The scroll! I still have it in my pocket from earlier. I never did have a chance to look at it, let alone decipher it."

Nova stood up at the king's high table on the dais, cleared away some of the dishes and plates and mugs around her, and unrolled the scroll that had been discovered in the spruce tree hollow. She flattened it out on the table on the dais. The Toad King glanced over her shoulder. Captain Grubbels walked forward to look on, and Juniper, Chordy, and Foxy crowded around.

"This is dire. Very dire, very grave, my friends," the Toad King muttered.

"What does it say?" Chordy grumbled. "We can't read it."

"It is a dispatch from a general of Alumbrial the Grave in the East, though it was not intended for our eyes. It may have been dropped by a messenger bird, one of the wrens of Alumbrial," the Toad King scanned the scroll rapidly. "It was a call to arms for the lands to the west of here, a bid to raise troops from the pine martens who live among the conifers, with an offer of great pay. Alumbrial has extraordinary resources at his disposal, it seems, if he is offering such a price. And there is some hint of his movements, here. They mean to seize Goldengrove by year's end," the Toad King let out a heavy sigh. "Ill news on the wind, my friends. Ill news for us all."

"There is a family of owls that used to live in the spruce tree hollow. I wonder if the wren dropped her message in a scrape with the owl family," Grubbels muttered. "But this is good luck, to have in our hands such intelligence from one of Alumbrial's generals."

"Here is my offer, Grubbels," Krub the Toad King bellowed out, suddenly. "I propose we forge an alliance between Sumbly and Riverbank. Divided we are easy victims for these warmongers that are laid loose upon our lands. But together we may stand some chance, however slim, of protecting Marchwood."

Captain Grubbels paused and nodded his head. "I cannot speak for all of Riverbank, and I won't speak out of turn. We must consult with Father Holbrook of the Order of the Munks, and our villagers. But I think you may be right. I have misjudged you, Krub. That I am freely willing to admit. But as for what our future will bring, none of us know. We shall hold a Council of War in Riverbank. But we must head back to the village and make arrangements, if you will agree to it. And I hope you shall, for it doesn't sound like have much time to waste."

"Indeed not, no, we have precious little time indeed. We shall be at your gates in the morning three days from now. A

Council of War will be held in Riverbank! *Briiibit!*" The Toad King croaked.

Nova, Juniper, Chordy, and Foxy gasped, as toads squeaked and croaked and chattered, and the village warriors of Riverbank broke into hasty conversation and murmuring. The quest to save their friend Rudbeck, which seemed so bold and daring an adventure in itself, had quickly opened their eyes to the greater world beyond the walls of Riverwood. It seemed that Marchwood was, in fact, at war.

PART TWO

CHAPTER 12

Preparations were being made for the Council of War in Riverbank Village. Rumors about the dispatch from Alumbrial's general—the message written on the scroll that Rudbeck had found in the spruce tree hollow—were spreading throughout Riverbank Village over every cup of tea and in every home. Everywhere throughout Riverbank village, the squirrels and mice and chipmunks and porcupines and rabbits could be seen standing on their porches and doorsteps and huddled in groups, chattering and talking, smoking their pipes, drinking their teas and brews, and working themselves into a flurry of worry and consternation over the grim forebodings of the past few days.

Over by the banks of the river, the lazy water wheel of the old mill turned in the steady current of the River Reed, grinding flour. At the top of the hill in the north of the village, a windmill turned around and around, overlooking the roots of the huts and tiny homes of the villagers. But now, the flour from the old mill by the river would be baked not into bread for evening feasts but for warriors' rations, and the inside of the windmill had been turned into a metal shaping facility to outfit armor, shields, and weapons for the villagers. At the gathering hall under the Meadow Tower, the older villagers repaired tattered and torn cloaks and blankets and packs to be taken on the march.

In a field in the southwest of the village, inside the walls, Captain Grubbels barked out orders to young creatures, drilling them in the use of the sword and shield: "One, two, three, *slash*! Step, step, and *stab*!" His voice boomed over the rooftops, and more than one of the cozy inhabitants of the once sleepy village of Riverbank shuttered their windows and shook their heads at the commotion.

Chef Goodknee was rolling a large barrel up the winding, overgrown stone path that led from the store rooms to the kitchens. Rudbeck was pulling a wagon loaded with casks and barrels and wooden boxes not far behind him.

"We should have built the store rooms closer to the kitchens. What were they thinking back in the day?" Chef Goodknee shook his good leg and stretched the bad one. "Come on, Rudbeck! Heave, pull, there's a good lad!"

Chef Goodknee started singing an old working song as he pushed the large wooden barrel up the hill, and a band of mouse children with small green and red and blue tunics scampered out from where they were playing in the blackberry bushes to help the old cook. Their voices joined in:

We can heave away, we can hack it out!
We can haul up, we can give a shout!
We can heave away, we can hack it out!
We can haul up, we can give a shout!

Weigh, hey, and up she rises!
Weigh, hey, and up she rises!
Weigh, hey, and up she rises!
Early in the morning!

The children laughed as they joined in with the chef, but several of them hopped into Rudbeck's already overloaded wagon and made the going harder for him. "Watch it, now, I can hardly manage it as it is," he huffed and puffed with labored breathing, and shooed the little mouse babes away.

Father Holbrook, the sagely elder chipmunk who was a leader among the Order of the Munks, the wise and academic chipmunks who resided mostly in the stone halls of the Riverbank Archives and spent their time in history and learning, walked calmly up the pathway, heading toward the gathering hall.

"Let me lend a hand, there, Goodknee. Rudbeck, you're young, you'll get there just fine." Holbrook stooped over and started pushed the great big barrel with Chef Kosta Goodknee. "Well, what do we have here today, Chef? What's in the barrel?"

Chef Goodknee panted but smiled at the chipmunk. "This here is one of my finest works, it's a double-black brew that's been aging in the cellars. This will be served at the council, to as many as it will allow, for our stout-of-heart warriors."

"You can call it the Riverbank Stout of Heart, that's not a bad name for a fine brew," Father Holbrook laughed. "You'll have to let me have a taste. It's been busier than I can ever remember. I worry about our little hamlet, here. I do worry," Father Holbrook wiped the sweat from the fur of his brow and kept on pushing.

"No need to worry, Father. They say the best army is a well-fed army, and there can't be a better-fed army in all of Marchwood than our very own, right here. Though I daresay the toad folk may not be too keen on my cooking. I understand they're accustomed to... well, a different sort of menu, that is."

"I have spoken with Grubbels at length," Father Holbrook reflected, "and apparently we have greatly misjudged the Toads of Sumbly Swamp. They are quite an educated and erudite lot, and they have kept their eyes peeled to the wider world much more than we have. They have important tales to tell and news to share with us at the Council of War this very day."

Father Holbrook and Chef Goodknee reached the door to the kitchens before long, and set down the barrel. The door to the kitchens was painted a rich, emerald green, but the paint was beginning to peel off, and the trim was loose around the door. A tarnished brass doorknob and an old pane of glass decorated the emerald door. Rudbeck came sweating and grunting up the path, pulling the overloaded wagon, which was creaking and groaning as he pulled it onto level ground just outside the door of the kitchens.

"Very good, Rudbeck! I don't suppose you want to stay and help with the meal prep? We'll have a few hundred to serve at the Council of War. There's about a thousand turnips that need peeling, and chopping, and the lettuce that needs washing, not to mention the tomatoes, cucumber, and onion for slicing. After that there's the fresh salted butter to be churned, and I haven't even started the main course, yet, or the deserts..."

"I'm quite occupied this afternoon, Chef, sorry to say. I've got to, erm, well I'm needed for training purposes. Have to practice my swordwork!" Rudbeck stammered out, then waved goodbye and dashed off in a hurry.

Father Holbrook and Chef Goodknee clasped each other around the shoulder and chuckled together, watching Rudbeck run down the stone path. Peeling a thousand turnips didn't sound like very much fun for Rudbeck, though the creatures of Riverbank usually didn't mind lending their help in the kitchens.

Many paws are strong together, the elders used to say.

"There's good folk in our village, my friend." Chef Goodknee reflected, smiling a big, honest grin. "Every single one of them."

"Aye, they're good folk, through and through. All the more that makes me fear for them." Father Holbrook replied, shaking his head in worry.

"No fear, my friend. It's courage we need, now. Courage more than anything. That's what I've learned through my days. Life can knock you and sock you about, break your bones, and even take your loved ones away. But no one can take your courage away from you. Face the day and face it strong, that's what I say. Ain't a soul in the world can take that away from you," Chef Goodknee mused, nodding to himself.

"Aye, aye... that is it, yes, my friend. Face the day. Though I'm not too certain what the days ahead will bring for us. We must face them."

As they stood there, lost in their ruminations, a shout rang out from the main gate of Riverbank Village. The procession of the Toad King of Sumbly Swamp was approaching

Riverbank, and the hour of the Council of War had come upon them.

CHAPTER 13

Krub, the Toad King of the black castle in Sumbly Swamp, was far ahead of his procession on the dewy path toward Riverbank Village. The toads had left before dawn of the third day since the meeting at the castle, and they hopped along at a fast pace, as toads can travel long distances at high speeds. Next to the king was his young son, Klab, who was the very same toad in the evening robe that had been sitting in the basement library just a few nights before at the toad king's black castle.

The two regal toads hopped along next to each other, eager to get on with their business. Long had they been waiting to meet with the Riverbank villagers to join their forces together. The three days between the odd events at the castle and the planned Council of War had proven to be strenuous on the aging king.

"Nothing so disturbs the spirit as coming to face the reality of evil in the woods," he had spoken to his son on the way. "One prefers to think of the woods in harmony, after all.

Though it is never so. It is always in change. *Change, change, change,* my son! Always *changing.*"

"Cannot change be harmonious, father?" Klab had remarked, thinking rather seriously about the topic.

His father had nodded gravely, saying, "Yes, yes. Very good, my dear boy. Very good, that is. Still, it's the *shifting* toward it and into the change that rakes my soul over. Everything must always be moving about. More's the pity," and his voice trailed off into a mumble and a croaking sound. They did not reprise the subject.

As the king's procession approached Riverbank, he noted with his astute and militaristic mind that the high walls were in places crumbling and sloping, and the treeline had grown in close in places to the walls. These were defensive defects that the Riverbank villagers hadn't noticed, due to their peaceful nature. They never imagined the serious possibility of an invasion; or at least no one had considered the serious possibility in several generations, or if they had raised any question about it, were told by the Order of the Munks that quarrying stone was a long and laborious business. A section of the wall had sunken down from the freezes and thaws of many winters. "This won't do one bit. They won't stand a chance," he muttered under his breath. "They're not ready for what is to come. Not ready at all."

The gates were thrown open for the Toad King, and the iron armored toads marched along the main pathway up toward the gathering hall. The soldiers of the Toad King's army made a frightful show to the peace-loving villagers of Riverbank, though none could look away, and children ran alongside the marching soldiers and elders looked out from the windows of their tiny stone homes and huts. The toad soldiers carried great, black banners with the emblem of the crescent moon, and wore aged but sturdy iron armor and helms, and stomped the ends of their long spears on the ground as they marched in unison. The toad captains wore long, black capes that blew in the breeze and made a striking impression on the villagers.

For their part, the Riverbank villagers had assembled a welcome committee, and Captain Grubbels and a band of his best warriors greeted the Toad King and his son as they entered the village, and walked beside them up the stone pathway toward the gathering hall. Grubbels had dusted off as many old uniforms as he could find, and fastened pins and decorations onto some of the more promising recruits, trying to give off the impression that his forces were well organized and ready for battle.

The pathway was winding, as it cut through the village square and rows of homes and shops and gardens. Krub the Toad King nodded as he looked left and right, surveying the village. He noted broken fencing in places and overgrown wildflower and bramble and burdock patches. "'Tis quicker to clean a castle than a town, my grandfather used to say. We have been lucky to have lived for so long and so comfortably in our castle in the swamp. Still, you have been rather contented in your years, here, haven't you?" The Toad King looked over to Grubbels.

"We may have let things go a little," Grubbels admitted, and patted his own overgrown belly. "Times have been good."

"Yes, and now we shall see the price to be paid," Krub the Toad King muttered.

But at that moment, the procession passed a great workshop, set up in a pole barn. The doors of the pole barn were thrown wide open to let in the breeze. Inside, Krub saw a flurry of activity, as soldiers sharpened blades and others hammered away at hot metal. "Perhaps there is hope," Krub croaked, smiling at Grubbels.

"Aye, we are quick to rise to the occasion. If only we had known. You cannot fault us for our happiness. Only, the heart grows fond of rest, and one is quick to dismiss the darker going-ons of the wider woods. We had forgotten what forces may be at work beyond our walls. You have opened my eyes, old... friend," Grubbels struggled to use the word, and twirled his mustache ends in his fingers. "Aye, you have opened my eyes, and we will rise to the day."

Tiny squirrel children in green and blue frocks ran alongside the marching toads, now, and gave them bunches of wildflowers tied up with strings of grass in pretty bows. The toads blinked and thanked them. One toad soldier placed the flowers in his helm proudly, and grinned goofily. Another of the toad soldiers slurped the flowers into his mouth with his long, wide, sticky tongue and swallowed them in a single gulp, having mistaken the gift for a snack. The squirrel children looked on in mock disgust and astonishment, then gave out big, deep belly-laughs. They had never seen folks from the swamplands before. In fact, the villagers of Riverbank had grown so restive, that most of them seldom left the gates and walls of their humble hamlet at all, unless they needed to.

The cracked, creaking wooden floor planks of the Riverbank Village gathering hall bowed and bent under the weight of the hundreds of creatures who piled into the space. King Krub and his son Klab went first into the hall, and the many creatures of Riverbank who were already there parted quickly to make way for the Toad King with his black iron crown and swishing black cape. He hopped along unaided, though he held a long, iron trident in one of his webbed hands that he sometimes used as a walking stick.

In the center of the room was a round table that had been set up especially for the Council of War. Biddy the herbalist, an elder chipmunk who had lived his whole life in Riverbank, had laid out a green table cloth and done his best, under Father Holbrook's direction, to make the proceedings look official and grand. Cushions were tied to wooden chairs, and an array of river stone candle holders, maps, and polished mugs were laid out. Though, it must be said, the maps of the Riverbank Villagers were not extensive and hardly covered the lands to the swamps to the north and halfway to the rich pine forests of the Shennan Valley in the West.

Father Holbrook stood up and welcomed the guests, while Captain Grubbels helped Krub and Klab take their seats. Also seated was King Krub's captain of the guards, a certain Brabbet Bilgar, who knew every detail of their forces and logistics. From Riverbank, Father Holbrook and Captain Grubbels were quickly elected to represent the village, along with the elder sage Glamdrill of the chipmunks, who was respected throughout the village as a great healer and wisest of the grandmothers.

Father Holbrook had promised that Nova, Juniper, Chordy, and Foxy could stand near the table to listen to the proceedings, though it was hard for them to squeeze through the throng of tightly packed animals to get near the table. Everyone in Riverbank wanted to hear the proceedings and to learn news from the wider Marchwood. Rumors had spread like wildfire about Alumbrial and the rogue Wolf of the North.

"Welcome, your highness, King Krub of Sumbly Swamps, and Klab, son of Krub, rightful and recognized heir," Father Holbrook bowed deeply. "I am father Holbrook, at your service." Father Holbrook was chosen to represent Riverbank Village, in part, because of his excellent manners and slow, deliberative nature.

The Toad King wasted no time, and began speaking before Holbrook had finished his greeting, "Father Holbrook, that's very kind of you," Krub sat down in his chair with a great thump, and the air pushed out of his lungs in a wheeze, "and I am entirely at your service, as well. I am glad to be present in your... mighty halls. But we must now face a grim reality. Alumbrial the Grave is sweeping through Marchwood and means to strike on Goldengrove by year's end. My own intelligence, which I have gathered carefully this spring, suggest his forces may equal ten thousand. Separated, we are no match for such an army. Together, we are still not strong enough to face such a foe, though our chances may be improved by working together. *Bribbt... bribbbbt...*" Krub the Toad King gave out a kind of toadish hiccup that interrupted his speech. "Ehm, excuse me. On top of this, your young Rudbeck and his friend Nova have intercepted a dispatch from the hollow of a spruce tree that we suspect was dropped by a messenger of Alumbrial. He means to ally his forces with the pine martens in Western Marchgrove. Our days here may be numbered if we do not craft a strategy with speed and tact," and with this the Toad King slammed his trident down onto the ground. "I do not mean to leave my home. *Bribbit.*"

Father Holbrook sat with his paws clasped in front of him, motionless, his white and blue robe trailing down nearly to his footpaws. He spoke, then, "The threats are now known to us, and we thank you humbly for your offer. Riverbank is rallied and roused. Though not everyone is in favor, I speak for my village and the majority. I move to ratify this treaty between our folks as soon as possible, so we may move on to our war plans. We are already arming. We are preparing for war. Though we do not know the way to succeed."

Krub the Toad King nodded gravely and smiled a curious smile, saying, "None know the way, and there are no certainties in this life, or any life, or any art or artifice of our endeavors. But this is a place to start." The king pushed across a carefully scripted parchment to Father Holbrook. It simply read as follows:

This treaty is to secure the peace between the Toads of Sumbly Swamp and the inhabitants of Riverbank Village in the lands of Marchwood, in their joint venture against the threat of invasion from Alumbrial the Grave. Amendments may be ratified at subsequent Councils of War to detail the plans of war and defense.

"I have no issue signing this pact, my friend," Father Holbrook muttered, and grabbed a porcupine quill pen from the table, dipped it into the rich blueberry ink that was so common in Riverbank, and signed his name at the bottom of the parchment. He passed the pen and paper over to Captain Grubbels for signing.

Captain Grubbels slammed his paw down on the table, "Very good, very good! But the problem lies in the planning! What chance do we stand against ten thousand? And what news of this rogue wolf from the mountains?" He signed the parchment nonchalantly and passed it back to the Toad King and his son.

The young red fox, who the friends all knew as Foxy, stepped forward, then, boldly. "I come from the East. I can tell you more about Alumbrial and the growing war..." he said.

"For the sake of the Great River, my boy, come and tell us!" and "Why didn't you speak sooner, lad?" they yelled in surprise, and the crowd parted to make way for the young fox to stand nearer to the circular table where the Council of War was unfolding in Riverbank.

CHAPTER 14

There was a great commotion in the gathering hall as the proceedings of the Council of War were interrupted by the young Foxy, the red fox who had come from the East and came to settle in Riverbank Village. Glamdrill the elder chipmunk and sagely grandmother of the village hushed the crowd.

"Come, this young one has seen the wars himself. He comes from the East. He surely has more to say than any of us, who only speculate on these affairs. Come and tell us what you have seen, my sweet one. You have many years in your eyes, though you are young," the sagely Glamdrill beckoned to him.

Foxy shuffled on his feet, the boldness going from him. Chef Goodknee, who was standing in the crowd just beside him and the friends, clapped him on the back with a heavy paw, and pushed him forward, "Go on, son! Be brave. That's what we're all saying, these days. These are strange times."

The red fox stammered, then started all at once in a rapid pace, "I came to Riverbank to escape the wars in the East.

There was a great battle near our fox den in the fields beyond Goldengrove, where we had settled years ago. My sister went missing in the battle. We were attacked all at once. It was said to be the work of Alumbrial, and I was separated from my parents. I went looking for them but nearly starved, so I headed out on the trails to find food and shelter. That's where I ran into one of the Order of the Munks on the road, a traveling pilgrim," Foxy took a deep breath in his hurried story.

"Yes, I met a traveling pilgrim, a chipmunk, like you folks. He told me to make for Riverbank Village, where there were others like him who lived in peace. And so it was, that you let me into the village, and I've been here ever since."

Father Holbrook nodded, and the Toad King blinked his eyes heavily and quickly. Father Holbrook leaned forward, intrigued by the fox's story, and asked him, "When was all of this? My memory leaves me more every day. It all blurs together in a fog. Tell us more, my son."

Foxy stepped forward, growing bolder and speaking more slowly and clearly, "This was just two weeks ago, if that. I haven't been here long. I didn't wait around to see if Alumbrial's soldiers would come back. They burned and hacked our gardens as they went. My sister's favorite raspberry patch..." he stopped himself, and looked down at his feet.

Nova and Juniper stepped forward and put their arms around him.

Nova the red squirrel spoke up, then, "He helped us save Rudbeck. He's a good companion and faithful to the village. We couldn't have tracked the toads without his help."

Grubbels slammed his fist on the big circular table again, as he enjoyed doing, and spoke out loudly, "Very well, no one is questioning the young fox's honor! We only want to learn more about this Alumbrial and what's happening in the East. What happened to his family's fox den may just as quickly happen here if we are not careful. These are dire times, indeed. Refugees in Riverbank! Pretenders to the throne hacking down berry bushes in the East! Rogue wolves in the North! We don't have a moment to spare, chaps!"

"Panic breeds nothing but more panic," Father Holbrook intoned warmly. "All our wits are here assembled, and we have news from our new friend, this young fox, that corroborates the intelligence of our guest, Krub, King of Toads.

We thank you for your stories, young one, and we will have more questions for you. Indeed, this puts everything into new perspective for us, as it confirms that Riverbank has truly been blind to the wider Marchwoods and their plight. There can be no question: Marchwood is at war. The question that faces me now is whether it is our duty to extend our help to the creatures of the greater woods, or whether our task is here at home, to watch our walls, repair our battlements, and train our creatures to defend themselves. It is not clear to me which pathway will lead to the greatest prosperity for our woodland folk. And it is not clear to me whether there is success down either road. Such is our plight," Father Holbrook scratched the black stripe on the top of his furry, fuzzy head.

Father Holbrook continued, "What we *can* do is begin by dividing our energies. The toads will patrol the lands around the Marchwood. Riverbank will send parties out to gather more information and to rally more forces. Even united, we are not strong enough to protect ourselves against ten thousand trained warriors. We need courageous young folk to assist us in this," the chipmunk continued. "Send this young fox, who knows so much of the unfolding war, and his friend

Nova the squirrel to the West to treat with the pine martens. Let us get to them before Alumbrial can pay them off. Their forces will join us."

Nova nodded her head sternly.

Glamdrill, the elderly sage, joined in, "And send our red hares to seek out the Great River. We have friends in the Southern Woods. Old friends. Good friends. Their fleet of galleys and fishing vessels and small craft may finally be put to good use."

"The Great River? You speak of myths and legends and lore, my dear," Father Holbrook shook his head. "You cannot be serious. Can you?"

Glamdrill nodded her head slowly, smiling. "Portents are more powerful than you might first imagine, Father Holbrook. I have long studied the ancient histories. We have before made friends with Mother Elm and the Roots of the World. If ever we needed to call again on our most sacred friends, the time is now."

The tales of village lore and the ancient histories of the dusty books of the archive told of the land known as the Roots of the World, beyond the Great River, where all life began. It was written that the tree of life, an old mother elm, there lived, among many strange creatures of the forest.

The Toad King croaked loud and long. "*Brrrrribbbbit.* Aye, aye. My toads shall patrol the forests and gather intelligence. For your safety, I will leave the largest part of my strength, a great cohort, in Riverbank to help defend your walls and keep your village at peace. And I shall stay stationed here and form a command center with my cabinet. We shall work together in these endeavors, my friends."

Captain Grubbels slammed his paw down on the table a final time. "Toads in Riverbank? Permanently stationed? While we send our best warriors out into the Marchwood? I won't hear of it."

"Now, now, Captain. We need all the help we can get. These are times for strong alliances and the bonds of friendship. Surely you can see that. We have misjudged our neighbors. We accept their help gladly. We cannot defend our walls alone," Father Holbrook added, trying to deescalate the tension.

The Toad King raised up the mug that had been placed on his table, and called for a toast to ratify their plan. Father

Holbrook signaled to Chef Goodknee, who filled all the mugs at the table with his double-black brew, which they had named the Riverbank Stout of Heart, and had been brought out especially for this momentous occasion.

They all clinked and clacked their mugs together, and took long drinks of the brew, as the Riverbank Villagers and the armored toads crowding outside the gathering hall cheered in unison, waving their hats and raising up a great cry, "Riverbank and Sumbly Swamps!" and "Down with Alumbrial!" and "Marchwood, Marchwood, Marchwood!"

Only Captain Grubbels looked displeased, twitching his mustache and looking suspiciously at the Toad King, Krub, and his son, Klab.

After the uproar died down, and villagers started to filter out of the gathering hall to begin their preparations for the patrols and voyages and training that had been decided upon, did Captain Grubbels raise his voice to address those who remained seated at the great circular table where they held the Council of War.

"I have a final condition I would like you to consider, your highness," Grubbels belted out, staring down the Toad King.

"Send your son Klab with my Western party that are heading out to treat with the pine martens in the Shennan Valley and the highlands. Klab's knowledge of the wider Marchwood will be most useful in our navigation, and it will do well to strengthen the bonds among this new generation of leaders, to have them adventuring together."

The Toad King croaked in sudden irritation, and his eyes blinked rapidly. "Very well, very good, my friend. We'll see to it." And the Toad King patted his son on the back with his webbed hand.

Klab, the toad prince, looked surprised, but perked up. "I look forward to the journey! Thank you for your suggestion, Captain."

The members of the Council of War all took one last drink and congratulated each other on the plans that had been set out before them. There was much to do in Riverbank Village and many long journeys that lay ahead of the parties that were to go out into the wider Marchwoods to seek for help among the friends of the forest.

Nova the squirrel, Juniper the rabbit, Chordy the porcupine, Rudbeck the mouse, and Foxy the red fox left the gathering hall quietly through a side door. They gathered in a circle in the tall grasses behind the old, wooden building and took in deep breaths of wildflowers and fresh air. The trees of the village towered over them. Further beyond, outside the walls of Riverbank, the great trees of Marchwood loomed higher still, creating a blanket-like, green and yellow billowing canopy in the distance.

"I don't suppose we'll see each other for a long while," Nova said.

"But more the merrier will we be when we are reunited. I'm lucky to have made such good friends," Foxy said, a bit nervously.

"Don't worry, me and Chordy will hold down the fort at Riverbank. I think we've had enough of the wide world for now. We'll make ourselves useful, here." Rudbeck put his arm around Chordy but yelped as he glanced one of the porcupine's sharp quills.

"I'll be heading to the West to find the pine martens with Foxy. We'll have to consult the maps. Juniper will be heading down the River Reed to seek out the Great River and ask for help from Mother Elm." Nova scratched her eyebrows. "You know, I always thought those were just tales for the little ones. Nice tales, for sure, but now I realize there's more to the ancient stories than I first had thought," she mused.

"Let's make a pact!" Foxy shouted suddenly. "We'll all meet back here by the end of the year. We'll cook a big feast just for ourselves and we'll bring in the new year together and talk about our adventures."

The friends all cheered up immensely at the thought of the happy days of hibernation in the long winters of Marchwood, when they would warm their toes by the fire and sip on warm, mulled drinks and teas and light their candles and hearth fires in their warm burrows and tiny stone homes. Nothing so pleased a Riverbank villager as the thought of a good, long hibernation with all the implements of coziness. The friends all put their paws into the middle of the circle.

"It's a deal," and "Great idea, Foxy!" and "Friends to the end!" they shouted, laughing and then raising their paws into the air all in unison.

They hugged, and went their separate ways. They didn't know when, and if, they would see each other again.

CHAPTER 15

Juniper the red rabbit and her family had long been interested in sailing and watercraft. Her family lived near the old watermill, and built small craft in a workshop down by the water's edge. On a sunny day, when the winds were just right, the rabbits could be seen fishing the wide waters of the River Reed on which Riverbank Village had been settled.

The great hare sailors of old had also left many larger vessels and a great galley, the flagship Rockpaw, which the rabbits kept stationed on the docks. In peacetime, its deck was more likely to be used as a dance hall. To be true, these larger ships had not gotten much use in many years, but the rabbits of Riverbank had kept them in good repair.

Juniper walked down the stone pathway that led to the river's edge, and waved to her family and friends who were already well into their work in preparing for the voyage. She loved to see friendly paws waving back. Everyone was busy, hauling lumber, pushing wheelbarrows, hammering, stirring pitch, or sawing planks by the banks of the River Reed. One small wooden craft was turned upside down, and a burly rabbit with long, floppy ears and a red smock was scraping the hull. Another rabbit, a young mother, was kneeling by the stern of a larger sailboat, inspecting and repairing a rudder that had clipped a stone in the shallows and been cracked.

Nilma Bramblepaw was the matriarch of the River Rabbit clan. Wearing a sailor cap—a round, flat hat that stayed firmly in place on the top of her head, as she had cut two holes for her ears to stand through—she strode confidently through the bustle of activity that dotted the shoreline of the River Reed. The water wheel on the old mill turned over and over, making a gentle splashing sound, and gentle waves slipped in and out on the white sands.

Above the sand line was dunegrass, which grew tall and green and sharp and high, next to which were seen the many shacks and shanties of the river rabbits that were built on the dune overlooking the river. It was nearly a village in itself, this settlement of rabbits by the river, with the tidily constructed tiny homes—for the rabbits were great woodworkers—and the running of the old mill, the many vegetable gardens, the workshops and well-stacked piles of lumber and materials and tools and barrels of nails and buckets of pitch all gave the impression of a well-ordered and self-sufficient folk who appreciated their work and enjoyed their labors.

You see, of course, that the old fables are mostly incorrect upon the matter of hares and their hastiness. The hare is not so hasty, after all, though they can work quickly, and sometimes stub their paws with the misplaced blow of a hammer. But in all, they are an industrious and meticulous folk who share a love of finely crafted things and a job well done.

Long piers extended out into the river. On the center dock, Nilma Bramblepaw now walked swiftly to and fro to inspect the craft that were there tied up and waiting at anchor. Juniper went to speak with her. Nilma paced about with her paws behind her back, muttering to herself incessantly.

"This will do. Yes, this will do. We've long awaited the day. We knew we would be called up. The day is long awaited..." Nilma trailed off, spinning about on her paws, and nearly bumped into Juniper.

"Hello there, my dear! What news?" Nilma asked.

"The fleet is to set sail before the Western party departs, or so the Order of the Munks and the Toad King have determined…" Juniper threw back her shoulders and tried to look smart as she spoke to Nilma Bramblepaw, who was voted unanimously as Admiral of the Fleet of the River Rabbits.

"Yes, so I've gathered from Piper Gaulik. I couldn't go myself to the council meetings, but he relayed the information to me. Too crowded. Too stuffy. You know what I always say," Nilma twitched her nose as she spoke.

"Fresh air, clean water, and more's the better!" Juniper laughed as she spoke the matriarch's famous words.

"That's right. There's a smart one," Nilma patted Juniper on the head. Juniper was very special to her, and Nilma always recognized and called to attention Juniper's brightness and gifted nature.

"I think you're ready to be in charge of your own craft, Juniper. It will be useful training for you to be in charge of one of the vessels in our fleet. What do you say? Are you up for the challenge, Captain Juniper?"

Juniper was astonished. "Why, yes, ma'am. Absolutely! Me, a captain?" She hopped in the air excitedly with her strong legs.

It was only a few days' time before the fleet was prepared. Hulls were mended and sails were patched, and crates filled with supplies, armors and arms, fishing spears, coils of rope, nets and daggers, and heaping barrels of Chef Goodknee's provisions were stowed onboard the boats of the river rabbits. The ancient tales of the Elm Mother were so varied and in such debate among the Order of the Munks that none knew exactly how long their voyage would take. They knew only they would be on the waters for a long while, as the River Reed flowed into the Great River, and from there into the old Roots of the World. Or, that was their plan based on their best knowledge from the archives and the old scrolls and books.

Nova and Foxy had come down to the dock to see Juniper off on her voyage. Many of the Riverbank villagers, including Father Holbrook, Chef Goodknee, and Mother Glamdrill had crowded around on the pier to wave their handkerchiefs and wish a safe voyage to the first of the expeditions to leave the village. The river rabbits were not a hasty folk, as has been said, but they knew they had little time to waste in seeking allies for the impending wars brewing in the East and the threat of Alumbrial the Grave that grew more real in their hearts every day.

It was a pleasant day as spring waxed fully onward and early summer started to rear itself with fresh blooms and deep greens in every tree. The sun beat down on the pebbles and sand on the banks of the River Reed, and dragonflies now fully grown danced in their incalculable patterns, zipping from stone to stalk and reed to dune. Beetles and baby grasshoppers scurried about in the dunegrass.

Juniper hugged Nova and Foxy, blinking back an excited tear.

"We've come a long way already, but we've a long way to go," Nova spoke quietly and encouragingly in her ear as they hugged. "And I know you can do it. Everyone keeps telling me to have courage, so that's what I'll say to you, too. There's nothing you can't do if you have courage in your heart. Just remember that." Nova smiled and blinked back her own welling tears.

Foxy grinned his big toothsome grinned and lightened the mood, saying, "Bring us back a regular army, won't you? I've been chatting with the chipmunks, you know, and they say there are all sorts of strange creatures in the Southern lands. There are cryptic messages in the old scrolls. Tell Mother Elm we say hello, won't you?" He began to laugh but Nova gave him a not-too-gentle elbow in the ribs.

"It's a very serious journey, Foxy," she reminded him.

"Of course, it really is. I'm not joking. Bring us reinforcements!"

"All aboard! Anchors aweigh! Last call, you landlubbers!" The matriarch sailor rabbit Admiral Nilma Bramblepaw shouted out over the waters from her large flagship at the head of the fleet, and Juniper hugged her friends a final time and ran off to hop onto her craft. She remembered always that moment, with the sun shining off the River Reed in bright, sparkly speckles, and the warm breeze of the air in her fur, and the faces of her friends waving their handkerchiefs on the shore.

The rabbits unfurled their sails and set off down the River Reed in their fleet of two score boats of all shapes and sizes, and colored sails and flags waving in the wind. Nilma Bramblepaw's flagship sped off, leading the way down the river. They began to sing all together:

Sails set to the sky, we stay true to our course
Together we shall make a mighty force!
Roll out the battle cry, upon the choppy waves
And forever in our hearts shall we be brave!

Anchors aweigh, my hares!
Anchors aweigh!
Feel the breezes in your ears
and the waves in all your bones
Anchors aweigh!
Anchors aweigh!
For long shall we be missing from our homes!

And we'll be alright if the wind is in our sails!
And we'll be alright if the sun is on our tails!
And we'll row the old chariot along!

Those who had come to watch the fleet sail down the river heard for a long while the sounds of commands shouted across the decks of the ships, the flapping of sails unfurled, and the splashing of waves churned up from the patchwork fleet of the red rabbits. The villagers, and even many of the armored toads, stopped waving their handkerchiefs as the fleet finally sailed out of sight down the River Reed, and turned to wiping the tears from their eyes with the handkerchiefs instead.

"I guess it's really happening, Foxy," Nova spoke her thoughts aloud. "The world's changing right before our eyes."

"Don't dwell too much on it. We're just along for the ride. And we're next to leave!"

The forty-some boats raced their waydown the river, and turned to black specks in the distance. Finally, the last of them turned a bend in the river, and they were gone from sight of the village, off to the great unknowns, to the lands that maps had long forgotten.

CHAPTER 16

The same day that the river rabbits sailed down the River Reed and off into the distance, Nova the red squirrel and Foxy the red fox took a long walk together through Riverbank Village. The day's busy preparations and flurry of activities had settled, and they ate a modest, slow-paced dinner picnic together on a checkered wool blanket in the orchard. They sat on the blanket, and Nova poured out her favorite Valerian root tea into two mugs and passed one over to Foxy.

The armored toad soldiers croaked rhythmically as they patrolled the wall-walk, high above on the battlements that encircled the town. The day turned to evening as the golden sun sank lower, at that peaceful time when one knows there is still an hour or two left before night, and everything is rich and warm and yellow and orange in the soft, fading light of those amber hours. Everywhere in the grass they heard tiny, black crickets chirping their newborn songs, filling the soundscape and mingling with the croaking of the toads on the walls and on the pathways. The presence of the soldiers and the steady activity of the village had become homey and comforting to Nova.

But Foxy was eager to leave. "Why wait for the company," he wondered, "when we're perfectly fit to go off adventuring ourselves? Don't you want to strike out on our own? Wouldn't it be more fun?"

"Oh, Foxy, you know Captain Grubbels has assigned us a troop, and besides, we need to take Klab with us. It's a special arrangement, to 'strengthen the bonds between our folk,' as they said. Besides, I am interested to learn more about the toad folk." Nova took a bite of a sandwich she had prepared at home, and, forgetting her manners at first, corrected course and handed the one she had made for Foxy over to him.

The red fox took a big bite. "Hot peppers and yellow onion and... what's this, a mature cheddar? You sure know how to eat right in Riverbank. You know, I have enjoyed my time here," he reflected, talking through the bites of his sandwich with his mouth full. "I had gotten pretty used to stale bread and weevil soup back at home. Supplies were running out, what with the war and all. I can't believe you were all just living here not knowing about the war. It's been such a big part of my life. Always running and hiding. But look where we are now."

"What's weevil soup?" Nova asked.

"I don't think you'd like it. Look, here's Klab coming, right now!" Foxy sputtered out in surprise.

It was in fact the young toad prince Klab, son of Krub, hopping along the path. Nova and Foxy waved him over to their picnic blanket in the orchard. Behind Klab swished a black cape in the wind, which he wore like his father, and he kept an iron trident in his webbed hand at all times, using it, as his father often did, as both walking stick and weapon.

"We were just talking about you, Klab. Wouldn't you like to go off tonight? We thought it would be more fun that way," Foxy patted the toad prince on the back. They had all become fast friends in the hustle and bustle of the war preparations since the Council of War had been held in the gathering hall.

The toad prince croaked happily, "That sounds marvelous, my friends. Allow me just the courtesy of notifying my father, and we shall be off right away. I don't suppose we can get off at once, can we? I have been rather eager myself to get our scouting started."

Foxy grinned his big grin. "A kindred spirit, I see. It's settled, then!" Foxy said, and put his arm around the toad prince in a friendly gesture.

Nova worried at the quick turn of events as the toad prince hopped off. She wasn't entirely convinced it was the right decision. But in a few minutes—before she could deliberate very extensively on the matter—Klab returned to their picnic spot. "I couldn't find my father, but I've left a note in his room at the barracks." The toad king and his son had taken up residence in a pole barn that had been converted into a barracks for the toad soldiers. "I can't think that he'll mind us leaving at all. I'm sure he'll applaud us for our aplomb and initiative. Though there's always a fine line between aplomb and audacity, wouldn't you say?"

Nova didn't quite catch his drift, but nodded her head and smiled. The three friends—Foxy, Nova, and Klab the toad prince—had made up their minds. Rather than wait for their party's departure, which was indeed slow in its preparation and always seemed to be delayed to depart, as the Riverbank soldiers needed much training, the friends were determined to set off that very evening through a side gate of the village and sneak off in the night undetected.

As those final few golden hours of the day departed and the sky turned purple and blue and red, the friends made their way to one of a few small gates built into the walls of Riverbank's defenses. They watched as two toad soldiers overhead marched by on the wall walk, croaking a marching song as they went.

"Well, the coast is clear! Let's get out of here!" Foxy rubbed his paws together in excitement.

"I'm not so sure, but I trust, at least, that this will be a great adventure. And I don't suppose I should be able to sleep, anyway, with all this excitement. Let's try for it! I trust in my friends." Nova whispered.

"Don't worry, Nova. I wrote it all down in the note. My father will make sure to notify Captain Grubbels and Father Holbrook and the rest. There's no need to worry. Let's just have a go of it. To the West, to the pine martens! We will be great diplomats! Ambassadors!" The toad prince liked the sound of these words: diplomat and ambassador. They had a regal and officious ring to them.

So the three sneaked off into the night, with the chirping of crickets and buzzing of evening's mosquitoes covering their trail as the small gate clapped shut behind them.

The smell of warm air and wet soil hit their noses as the three hurried off over the fields and across the ditches, over a small stone bridge that carried them over the meadow stream, and into the dense treeline to the west of Riverbank Village.

"I don't know the paths well, Foxy. But I appreciate your tracking skills. You took us to Klab's castle, after all. And you told us the story about your sword. Or part of it." Nova glanced at the curious and powerful looking broad sword that Foxy kept at all times in its scabbard slung across his back. She glanced at the toad prince, then. "You know, sorry about that whole mix-up in the library. We were trying to save our friend!"

"Forget all about it, it's over and done," Klab the toad prince croaked. "I also know these woods well enough. I've been on voyages here and there with my father and our guards through the years. A toad doesn't do too well sitting at home all the time. The tongue grows restless, as they say," he smacked his long, toadish tongue over his lips, "and the bugs need mowing down. In fact we were in these parts not too long ago hunting locust. They were numerous two, maybe three years ago. That was a very hot summer, which had something to do with it, I suspect. There were absolute *swarms* of them, and bigger than you can imagine." The toad prince shuddered in pleasure. "Tasty, too."

A bright red cardinal flew over their heads, chased by another just behind it.

"Spring in the Marchwoods, that is. Though it won't be long 'til summer," Nova sighed happily.

The three ventured on into the night, as the stars came out and the air grew cooler. The stillness of the woods at night comforted them rather than spooked them, though their legs and their eyes and minds grew weary from the tramping and stamping through the understory and brush of the dense forest of the West.

They came upon a ravine with a small stream, thick with last autumn's leaves underfoot.

"We can stop here and make a small fire," Foxy thought aloud. "It looks plenty peaceful and quiet to me. I can't imagine we'll be bothered. Krub, Nova, do you reckon there's any risk in lighting a fire?"

Krub nodded his head, "I'm plenty hungry. We always make camp with a fire to warm our toes, when I'm traveling with my guards, though we do not always need it to cook. Some things are better raw and wriggling," he said. "Then again, we are large in number when we go on patrol, and there is just the three of us."

"I should feel safer and warmer with a fire," Nova said, "and I can't think it will do much harm. We're still within a stone's throw of the village."

So they made camp for the night under the birch trees and warmed themselves by the fire, covering themselves with blankets and sleeping on the soft leaves. Krub soon fell asleep and was snoring a toadish snore, his tongue lolling and falling out of his mouth, but Foxy and Nova rested their arms behind their heads and used their rucksacks as pillows, looking up through the branches at the starry night sky.

"Do you ever wonder what's out there? Or up there? I should like to go to the moon." Nova said.

"In Goldengrove they say the moon is full of craters and holes from great falling stars smashing into it. Or something like that. But it's so far away, we couldn't get there." Foxy whispered back.

"Mother Glamdrill always told me the moon was the child of the world, and the world was the child of the sun, though I don't know how true it is," Nova said back to him, dropping her own voice to a gentle whisper.

"It sounds nice. It's nice to think those sorts of things, I think. It helps me sleep at night, anyway. I wouldn't want to think there weren't any reason for us to be here, you know?" Foxy yawned and turned over.

"There's always a reason to be here, Foxy. We have friends and family and the woods and the stars, fire and food, and stories to tell. And we have an *adventure* to go on—a very important adventure. There's always a reason to keep going, even if we don't understand why, or we don't now the way, or we're confused about the bigger picture..." Nova got excited by her own philosophizing, but when she looked over at her friend, she saw his chest rising and falling as if in a deep sleep, and he started to snore.

A father owl, who was sitting up in the hollow of a mature oak tree, watched over his family of owlets and his owl wife who slept next to her babies, keeping them warm. The father owl peered out from the hollow and watched over the three travelers below, feeling content in doing his part as lookout.

CHAPTER 17

Juniper had fully settled into the captaincy of her small craft, which she named the Waterwheel, after the old, tumbling water wheel of the mill near the home where she grew up in Riverbank Village. She was always comforted by the steady rhythm of its turning, circular motion and the sound it made splashing regularly and powerfully in the water. The June sun cast its bright midday rays down on her fur, which warmed her all over, and she closed her eyes and steadied the rudder. Spray from the River Reed splashed her whiskers and she smiled at the fresh air and sun and droplets spraying up from the craft bobbing up and down in the currents.

Upon her craft—which was none too measly for her first official stewardship of a river-ready boat—were ten crew members and soldiers, mostly youngsters who were on their first voyage as well. But the deck boss, a bosun named Bale, was getting a little too carried away with her role.

"Now, now, fasten those ropes nice and tight!" The deck boss yelled out. "We don't want any barrels going over the edge. Then you'll be sorry! You want to eat dinner, don't you?"

"Bosun Bale! Let's take it easy on the new recruits. There's no reason we can't enjoy the float. It's a beautiful day. Let's get some grub up on deck, and some fresh grog for everyone," Juniper called out in a singsong tone that cut clear over the rush of the water.

"Hooray for Cap'n Juni!" the crew all cheered, and threw up their arms.

"Fair enough, my dear!" Bale went below deck with two of the crew to fetch the mid-day lunch. The sun was high overhead and there wasn't a cloud in the sky.

Below deck, Juniper heard a yell and fumbling about, and Bale came running back above deck from the stairs that went below. Stuck in her paw was a massive porcupine quill. "Stowaways! Invasion! Mutiny! Murder!" she yelled out.

Juniper laughed as she saw the stout, heavy frame of her friend Chordy emerge from below decks.

"Calm down, everyone. This is my good pal, Chordy. Though I don't know what you're doing on my ship! Explain yourself, my friend," Juniper ran over to him and gave him a warming hug.

"Poor Bale there must have mistook me for a turnip and tater pie. I was just having a nap in the larder. I snuggled up on top of a sack of flour, and next thing you know, I was fast asleep, and the fleet sailed off. I did very much wish to join you, though. I love a good adventure, and I couldn't stand waiting back at Riverbank while you and Nova and everyone went off on your travels. It just didn't seem right to have you going off without me," Chordy said. "And well, now look at me. I'm a sailor!" He put one hand on his hip proudly. In the other hand he still carried the great poleaxe with him, which he gripped tightly.

"We'll make a sailor out of you, alright. We're to have lunch, now, but you know there's a lot of work on a boat. There's scrubbing and hoisting and hammering and cooking and cleaning and mending and steering and navigating..." Juniper stopped as she noticed her friend had turned away and had grabbed a handful of biscuits from a rabbit passing by with a massive plate.

"I like this ship of yours, Juniper. Top notch service, even."

The day passed on like that, with Chordy and Juniper chatting away, and everyone doing their level best to get accustomed to life on the River Reed. Little navigation was needed in this area as the river straightened and broadened and moved them nearly due south for miles and miles.

Sometime in the late afternoon, the scent of the air shifted, and a dewy wetness caught Juniper's keen nose. "There's a change in the air, Bale. Do you smell it?"

"Aye, I do, and you're keen to point it out. And look there, over the hills. It's looking dark. It'll likely miss us, but we best get everything fastened down just in case."

Juniper grew nervous as she noticed the other vessels in the fleet furling their sails and wrapping them tight.

"Nothing worse than a loose jib in a high wind, deary," the bosun commented, but Juniper only pretended to nod in understanding, not fully knowing yet the danger that lay ahead.

A booming crack of thunder from far in the distance rolled out over the warm, June air, and half the crew jumped where they stood. The massive gray cloud over the hill picked up speed and seemed headed right for them, and Juniper could see in the far-off hills the sheets of raining falling from the cloud, and flashes of pink and red lightning bouncing from one tower cloud to another like strobes.

There was a greenish tint to the belly of the clouds that made Nilma—Admiral Nilma of the River Reed Fleet—nervous as she walked the deck on the flagship, The Rockpaw. The flagship was the largest of the vessels, sailing just behind two smaller craft that were acting as scouts. Admiral Nilma stood on her quarter deck and looked up to the green clouds and then backward over the rail, scanning her fleet. She could practically smell the danger blowing in the wind.

On her own ship, Juniper suddenly found herself growing into a leading role. "Listen here, everyone! I don't like the look of that storm, if my senses know anything. I want all sails fastened tight and roped up as well as you can manage, and I want every last bit of cargo fastened down below deck. And I don't want anyone going overboard—make sure there's plenty of lifeline, the best rope we have, ready to go." Juniper looked up above her. "Hayby, you come down from the lookout! It's not safe up there. You've been relieved of your watch until the storm passes!" On the main mast, the young rabbit named Hayby started descending from the crow's nest.

A flash of lightning came, closer this time, and a crack of thunder rolled through the waters, and every rabbit aboard the fleet perked up their ears as a natural reflex. The edge of the storm grew closer and sheets of rain were falling, the sky completely dark overhead. The waves began splashing and thrashing about, and the sailors worked their best to separate the ships from slamming into one another.

The storm was coming!

CHAPTER 18

In the Western Woods, Foxy, Nova, and Klab woke up the next day in their campsite. In the night, they had heard the distant booms of far-away thunder, but they had stayed perfectly dry in the gully with their blankets and rucksacks as pillows as the warm embers of the fire burned low in the night. The storm was far off from where they ventured. The father owl who had—unbeknownst to the travelers—kept a lookout through the night, was now getting his daytime rest, as tiny owlets snoozed in and out of morning sleep.

The three friends rose early and drank cups of fresh water from the stream that passed through the gully in which they had made their simple camp. Foxy rolled up his blanket quickly and tied it below his pack, and Klab overturned a log to snack on the "bright bugs of morning," as he referred to them.

"Suppose you wouldn't want a mouthful?" Klab asked Nova, crunching on the shells, a wing and a leg sticking out from the side of his mouth.

"Oh, that's fine, thank you, Klab." Nova's eyebrows raised instinctively, and she put down her breakfast roll and stood up. "I think it's probably time we get a move on. These morning hours are nice and cool and we can put a lot of miles behind us."

"Westward bound!" Foxy yipped excitedly.

The three travelers put many miles behind them, indeed, in the morning light of the Western Marchwood. The trail was ancient, and in parts was in disrepair. There was almost no traffic between the settlements of the West and Riverbank Village.

"Why don't the pine martens come over to Riverbank?" Foxy asked.

"We were never much for trading and mercantilism. We've always been self-sufficient. Though it's got me wondering if we should have kept better relations with our neighbors in the woods. Here, all this time, we've had good friends in the toads, not more than a day's march from our home. I wonder how the pine martens will find us."

"They shall find us as friends, I should hope," Foxy said, though he wasn't too sure of himself.

The land grew higher and the friends found themselves walking uphill, almost climbing in spots, as the trail turned into steep inclines. On one side of them was a deep gully, and the path was narrow and uneven. In places, they had to jump over fallen logs and watery ditches in the path.

As the land inclined and they found themselves winding higher and higher up the twirling paths in the forested hills, they noted the trees were now mostly tall pines and old pines that grew far overhead. Last year's pinecones had fallen all over the trail, and they had to watch where they stepped. It doesn't do well to step on a pointy pinecone, unless you want sharp bits stuck in your paws.

The path kept winding higher and higher into the rocky pine forest, until the land looked very different from where they had began in the meadows by the village. The path eventually leveled out at the top of a large hill, and broke off in a few different directions. One short tributary of the path went straight to a rocky outcropping, where a massive stone was lodged in the side of the hill.

Nova, Foxy, and Klab scrambled up the stone and stood on its high, level top. From there, they could see for miles and miles to the east, and somewhat to the north. Nova scanned the greens and yellows and blues of the trees and fields, but everything looked so far away, it nearly blended together. She spied, then, the great Northern Mountains, far, far off in the distance, towering there like gray monoliths with their white peaks. Down from those mountains flowed the River Reed, and she followed the line as it emerged out from the thick forest and wound its way through the land. She saw, then, not incredibly far away from them, the stone walls of Riverbank Village nestled there by the River Reed. She tried to look behind her, to the south, but the forested hilltop blocked her view in that direction.

"Oh! I know which hill we are on, now. It's just one of the Three Ladies, as we call them. You can see them on a clear day from the Meadow Tower in the village. I used to climb up in the Meadow Tower to have my tea when I was a bit younger." Nova remembered. She enjoyed "putting the pieces together," as she called it—that is, gathering her bearings.

"I wonder how Juniper is getting along on the river," Foxy wondered. "There was a storm that way last night, I think. Did you hear the thunder?"

To their left, not far off to the north, they saw a swarm of white gulls flying in circles. Further off Nova thought she saw a crow, or maybe a raven. Sage Glamdrill had tried to teach her all the birds of Marchwood when she was younger, but she struggled to connect the names with the descriptions, especially not having seen many of them. She remembered ravens were quite larger and usually did not travel in groups. Perhaps it was a raven, after all. Or perhaps a crow on its way to meet her friends.

From up there, time and life felt different. Down below were the castles and towns and folks and creatures moving around, going about their business. From above, it somehow seemed both more and less important. Houses might be built and castles might crumble, but the woods would always be there. Days would come and go, the moon would rise and set, over and over and over again, Nova realized in that moment. Though it was still early in the day, she imagined the sky turning dark and the moon rising and arcing across the sky, then setting, then rising, then setting, then rising, over and over again, in a steady and consistent whirl. She didn't feel small; rather, she realized that *everything* was small, and that was somehow comforting from the vantage point of the hilltop.

Foxy seemed to read her thoughts, as he said, then, "Look, there's the day-moon rising!"

It was in fact the moon, just a day or two from its full shape, rising over the hills.

"I always love that about the moon. You never know where she'll come up. The sun is so predictable. But the moon... you never know," Foxy whispered, amazed at seeing the white shape in the blue sky looming large in the far hills off on the horizon. Seeing the moon in the daytime was a pleasure shared by Nova and Foxy, and many of the woodland creatures of Marchwood.

"The chipmunks have studied the patterns. They've made records of when and where it comes and goes, and can predict where it will be. But they're not sure exactly *why*," Nova said.

"Well, they ought to find out! I'd like to know," Klab laughed. "Perhaps she has a mind of her own. That would be a fine thing." Klab stared longingly at the white moon in the bright, blue day. He waxed on, "In toadish lore, the moon is the keeper of tongues and patroness of the freedom of speech.

They say when the moon is out, a toad can speak their mind more freely. The moon reminds us to be honest and true. Long ago, the sun stole the tongues of the toads, and kept them in his kingdom, because he was jealous of our songs. But the moon rose in the sky and crossed his path. She blocked the light of the sun, stole back our tongues, and restored them to our throats." Klab still looked at the moon as he spoke, and it was now rising higher over the hills. "Of course it is all nonsense and folklore, but we love those kinds of stories. There is nothing wrong to be reminded that every creature should always have the freedom of their tongue, to say as they think, and think as they please, as long as it is in the pursuit of what is true and just and good." Klab put his hands on his hips, pleased with his summary of this important bit of spiritual and philosophical toadism.

Nova had never heard this story, and quite enjoyed it. "That's quite nice, Klab. They do say the moon passes over the sun, sometimes, and blocks its light. Have you heard that, Foxy? I've never seen it, an eclipse. Maybe someday."

Foxy nodded, "I've heard others say the same. My father said..." Foxy choked back his words.

"What is it?" Nova asked.

"My father said the night that Alumbrial was born, there was such an eclipse. When the moon stole over the sun. I don't know if it's true. I don't like to think about what's happening, that way." Foxy said. "I don't like to think about it."

Nova had forgotten that they were looking toward the lands of the East. Though they could see far, they could not see forever. And somewhere beyond their sight, they knew that somewhere, off in the hazy blues and greens of the world, there was the city of Goldengrove and its many settlements. And somewhere out there was Foxy's family, waiting to be reunited with him.

"We better be off on our way. We have our alliance to forge with the pine martens!" Nova said, patting his back. "We'll find your family, again. I know we will."

And so the three travelers descended the stone at the top of the hill, and made their way back onto the winding path through the pine forest, in search of the martens who they hoped to make their allies.

CHAPTER 19

At Riverbank Village, the presence of the toad guards, who were at first so welcomed by the villagers, had begun to drain the patience and resources of the sleepy, little riverside hamlet. The toads were voracious eaters, and ate three times as much as a full-grown mouse or squirrel. They had brought enormous wagons full of barrels of their toad grog—a kind of acidic mash that smelled of corn and yeast and heavy fumes—which they consumed throughout most of the day, and smoked enormous amounts of marsh tobacco from their twisted, twirling, wooden pipes of hardwood and iron. They were a rowdy bunch, and many of the elder villagers took issue with their unfamiliar ways.

It was not uncommon in those days and weeks following the Council of War to wake up early in the morning, look out of one's windows, and find a knot of toads sleeping in one's front lawn. (For it soon became known to the villagers that a pack of toads is called *a knot*.) Father Holbrook more than once had to shoo drowsy toads from the front steps of the archives, where he worked with other chipmunks in the mornings, poring over maps and ancient histories. This clashing of cultures was mostly, however, boiled down to a simple misunderstanding—for the village creatures kept their waking hours in the light of day, while the toads preferred to keep their waking hours in the dark of night.

As the toads got settled into village life, Captain Grubbels more seriously took up the part of drill sergeant, trying his level best to train the warriors into a full, fighting force. Rudbeck the mouse did not perform well under Captain Grubbels's training regimen. "I'm a good adventurer, and quick on my paws, but the military life isn't for me!" He quickly decided, after the second week of sunrise drills and hundreds of laps around the pond. It was a hard decision, as Captain Grubbels had been like a grandfather to Rudbeck for most of his life, and took him under his wing. Still, Rudbeck chose instead to break off on his own to learn more about the toads and see if their ways might suit him better. After all, they did appear to be having a lot more fun, with their barrack halls teeming with food and drink, their massive tents filled with music and hanging lanterns, and the late-night revelries of feasting and sporting and dancing.

Rudbeck was not alone in his curiosity. Many other of the younger—and some of the older—villagers took a real liking to the foreign toads, and befriended them instantly. They learned how to dance The Whip-Tongue Jig, The Low-Marsh Fling, and the High-Hop Two-Step on the wooden platform erected under the main dance tent. The toads, for their part, learned new songs like "The River Reed Shanty" and the "Nightowl Blues," and shook their webbed toes and snapped their fingers to the unfamiliar beats and melodies. It was a melding of worlds under the canopies of these tents, late at night. The accordions, bone whistles, and drums of the toads blended harmoniously with the hurdy-gurdies, meadow horns, and ocarinas of the villagers. Grogs and ales and brews and wines were passed around freely late into the night, and lanterns hung from inside the dance tent, giving off a warm glow and peaceful, enchanting atmosphere.

That night, Rudbeck sat on a picnic table freshly built from cedar. The toads had set to work right away making the village comfortable for themselves. They enjoyed working with wood, and learned much—and learned quickly—from the craftsfolk of the village. Some of the toads even began helping to mend fences and crooked doors. Rudbeck held a big clay tea mug in his paws that he had repurposed as a party cup. It was filled with Chef Goodknee's strong Stout of Heart brew, a double-black stout that curled the whiskers and warmed the toes. Chef Goodknee had set to work brewing barrel after barrel as the compliments rang in after the brew was served at the Council of War. It was a real success, and helped warm relations between new friends and the bellies of the watchguards who patrolled the wall walk and battlements from dawn to dusk.

Next to Rudbeck on the picnic table was a soldier toad in a black cape and evening dress: a black tunic buttoned up with silver buttons to the collar. A sword hung from a scabbard at his side. He wore a black cap and black gloves. Rudbeck was deep in his cups already, though the night had just turned dark.

"I still say, why all the *black*, Bargles? Everything is the color *black* with you toads. Black capes and black gloves and black caps. Black isn't even a color," he stammered. "It's the anit-color, the opposite of color. Why not some *yellow*? A simple splash of *color*! You would look dashing in some moss green and forest hues. It would match your skin tone!" Rudbeck waved his arms around excitedly.

The toad, Bargles, croaked a big belly laugh and swigged back more of his brew. "You'll have to fetch me a new outfit, Rudbeck. I'll wear it just for you. Make me look like a flower! Dress me up like a dandelion!" They both laughed together.

Their laughter stopped when they heard a ruckus break out on the dance floor. They heard the scraping of steel on scabbard, swords being drawn, and shouts of alarm.

Rudbeck and Bargles jumped up on their table to see what was going on.

Under the dance tent, a group of porcupines rattled their quills and pointed fingers at an armored toad guard. "He shoved me, he knocked me over!" A porcupine with a feathered cap shook his finger in a rage. "These toads are no good for our village, they're eatin' all our food and sleepin' on our doorsteps and making a ruckus!"

Rudbeck and Bargles jumped down from the table and walked confidently over to the scene of the confusion.

"Now, now, Durny, there's no need to be prejudicial." Rudbeck exclaimed to the unhappy porcupine. "These toads are our friends. They watch our walls! They keep us company! They mend our fences!" Rudbeck the mouse put his arm around his toad friend, Bargles. "See, look. This is how you treat a toad. You love 'em and welcome 'em into your arms!"

"We'll see about that," Durny the porcupine muttered under his breath. He walked away, waving his paws at his porcupine friends, and they all followed.

"I don't think that's quite settled, yet, Bargles." Rudbeck shook his head in worry.

"There's nothing that so grieves me as creatures who can't get along." Bargles sighed.

The next day, the tension between the toads and the Riverbank villagers reached a breaking point. Krub, the Toad King, was bellowing and croaking in a fury in the main barracks. The note that Klab had left, alerting to him to their plan to leave the village ahead of the expeditionary forces, had been accidentally filed away by a captain of the guards, so that Krub never hda a chance to read it. Because of this, no one in Riverbank knew the whereabouts of Nova, Foxy, and the toad prince, Klab.

Krub stormed out of the barracks and confronted Father Holbrook at his morning work in the archives.

"My son is missing, and today is the day we are to set out to the West! Explain yourself, Father Holbrook! What trick has been played on my people? You have taken my son hostage, or imprisoned him, I assume!" The Toad King, Krub, puffed his cheeks and chest out in a rage.

"I have not seen your son, the prince Klab..." Father Holbrook looked up from his research. His desk was a scattered but organized assortment of papers, books, parchments, and scraps of notes.

"I do not think kindly of this! I do not think kindly of this at all!" The Toad King stormed out of the archives, assuming the worst, and setting a dark mood. The expeditionary force that was to follow westerly out of Riverbank that very morning was put to a halt, and search parties were formed to discover the whereabouts of the toad prince, who had, of course, simply left the village early with his friends. Krub was determined not to leave the village until his son had been found.

CHAPTER 20

The fleet of Admiral Nilma Bramblepaw was rocked and bashed by the waves of the unexpected storm that came down upon the two score vessels making their way southerly on the River Reed. She had to use the full skills of her soul to keep the flagship afloat and to do what she could to steer her fleet through the raging blasts of the waves and the thundering storm.

Aboard the flagship, the Rockpaw, Admiral Nilma braced herself on the quarterdeck, looking backward at the fleet. She looked on in dismay as she saw her fleet of ships struggling in the growing storm, rocked by waves, bashing their hulls against one another. Two smaller craft had managed to get ashore, and she faintly saw some of her sailors abandon their ships to the storm and run off into the woods.

"Yellow bellies!" She yelled to herself, as none could hear over the storm. "Or they're smarter than we are, maybe. This is a fine mess if I've ever seen one." Admiral Nilma went into the captain's cabin to refill her silver stein of the good, double grog that they had provisioned in the ship. "Might as well have one last drink to drain it all down. Maybe an idea will come to me, down here." She filled the stein from her private cask, and wondered why she didn't order a few casks of good, red berry wine for her stash.

Just as sheets of rain were drenching the sailors aboard Juniper's ship, Juniper managed to get her wits about her and order the oars and longpoles to be brought up from belowdecks.

"Push to the shore!" She shouted over the din, the rain battering her and the sheer darkness of the storm clouding her vision. She could hardly see across the deck of her ship, with the torrents of rain and the waves splashing and battering over the railings. Dark, wrathful clouds of grayest grays and greenish black powered by, far overhead, blocking out all but little light.

The waters were too deep, and try as they might, the sailors aboard the ship could not reach the bottom of the river, and tried in vain to steer the ship to shore so they could anchor and find cover in the woods.

In the raging of the storm, that fleet had become jumbled together, and ships smashed into one another from every angle as they were rocked about by the turbulent waters. Waves crashed over decks and boards splintered and groaned and masts became tangled in the maelstrom.

Chordy was using a longpole to push with the full might of his heavy frame against another ship that had come too close to the Waterwheel. The Waterwheel was the name of Captain Juniper's ship, which she had named after the water wheel of the peaceful mill near where she had grown up on the banks of the River Reed. Her village and her cozy life at home now seemed a far way away, as lightning snapped and thunder cracked and roared across the deck. More than once she wondered what she had gotten herself into.

"Over here, over here!" Chordy shouted, and the crew gathered round to use their poles and oars to try to push the ship next to the Waterwheel away from their hull, but the waves kept battering and battering and soon sent the other boat scraping and plowing into the Waterwheel. The two ships slammed together, side to side, knocking Juniper off her feet and onto her paws and knees.

"We need the sails, captain! Unfurl the sails! We've got to get out of here! We won't have any use for a mast if we don't have our lives!" A stout and grizzled hare named Garnum with a long beard shouted through the storm. The bosun Bale yelled in agreement. "Let loose the sails, let them fly!"

"We can't risk losing the mast! It'll break in the winds! Our sails will be tattered!" Juniper cried out. She ran across the deck, looking to and fro, trying to help where she could.

Garnum stepped up to her, and put his bearded face just an inch from hers. "We'll lose our lives, here, captain! We need the sails to blow ourselves out of this mess! Look at the fleet, it's going to be wrecked!"

Juniper shook her head and almost gave into the thought, when a great wave rocked the ship from side to side and the sailors slipped on the watery deck. She watched in fear as she saw Chordy the porcupine, her good friend and stowaway on the ship, fly over the railings and into the water below.

"Overboard! We've lost Chordy! Overboard! Help, help!" Garnum tried throwing a line over the side of the Waterwheel, but just then, another great wave pushed the other ship into its side, and an ear-splitting *crack* and mournful groan of timber, as of a thousand trees falling over at once, racked and rent through the hull of the Waterwheel.

Juniper lost all vision and sense of surrounding as water and wood and iron and sail flew up into the air around her in a flurry of confusion, and she felt a whumping *thump* on the back of her head and lost consciousness.

CHAPTER 21

The Western party—that is, Nova the red squirrel, Foxy the red fox, and Klab the toad prince—put many miles behind them, day after day. The days then turned into weeks, and May turned to June, and the days grew longer. The pine groves and hills of the West country extended for unfathomable miles, and Nova wondered at how she had never known that such a vast, rocky, hilly, and extraordinary land could lay so close to her home and she had never known it. Now, the world was transforming from the unknown into the known before her very eyes. Her world was widening with every step that she took further away from the place where she grew up.

Finally, after nearly a month of marching, camping, exploring, and eating, the three friends—a bit worn from the wear of the road—came upon a valley that descended down from the rocky, pine-covered hills from which they looked.

"Down there, look!" Foxy shouted.

Below them in the valley was a forest village like they had never seen. In the tall pines, there were houses built into the branches on platforms, and strings of lanterns were strung from branch to branch and winding up the trunks of the massive trees. Rope bridges were strung between the trees, and they watched as tiny figures—far away as they were—moved about in activity in the city in the forest, deep in the valley. They noticed a stream cut through the center of the forest city. Settlements of tiny homes, cabins, halls, shops, libraries, towers, and all manner of strange and exciting buildings rose up among the trees and gardens and winding stone roads of the valley city below them.

"That must be where the pine martens live! And they've got freshwater running through there, by the looks of it. I reckon we could use a quick bath." Foxy sniffed himself, and turned his nose in Nova's direction, but she pulled away before he could smell her. "Suit yourself," he said.

The worn travelers did what they could to brush themselves off and straighten their caps and tunics and cloaks and clothing, and Foxy tried brushing the old battered uniform he wore with the back of his paw, and straightened his collar, as the three descended from the rocky hills into the forested valley of the martens.

The narrow, dirt path quickly widened, and intricate stonework now paved the ground underneath their paws. The stone path built by the martens cut through the hilly terrain and over ravines, and arched bridges of stone with skillfully carved and tasteful ornament dotted the hillside. They passed over many of these stone bridges, and stopped, leaning over their sides, to marvel at the beauty of the forest valley. At one such bridge, a waterfall cascaded down the side of the rocky hills and tumbled far down below, and they felt the splash of water as they leaned over the edge.

"This is a wondrous country," Klab marveled. "Look at the fish jumping," he pointed down the waterfall. Red river salmon splashed their way over the gentle falls to the streams below, and jumped among the shining rocks and white foam of the fresh, cool, water. "What more does one need than warm breezes and fresh water?"

"Warm breezes, fresh water, and fresh salmon!" A powerful, baritone voice boomed out across the bridge at them.

At the far end of the stone bridge, a massive brown bear stood towering over them, taller by twice than even Foxy, who was a good height for a young fox. The brown bear wore country attire, a tweed coat with a white undershirt unbuttoned to the chest underneath, and he seemed to have an other-worldly air about him that Nova couldn't quite place. He wore high, brown, back-country boots. Around his head his hair had grown long, almost like a mane, and about his chin and neck was a fuzzy, ferocious beard that was without order and entirely wild. On his head he wore a patchwork, ivy tweed wool cap of many colors and patterns stitched together.

"Don't be alarmed, my friends. I'm only doing some fishing. I'm on vacation." They noticed then the thick, long cigar trailing smoke from his paw. He took a long puff of the light, airy smoke and then took a deep breath, filling up his lungs, and then letting it all pour out his chest. He looked quite happy. "Yes, I'm on vacation, finally. A most *reverent* and much-needed vacation. Are you on your way to Shennan Valley? It's not long off, now, and the road doesn't wander."

The brown bear walked slowly over to the three friends and leaned over the side of the bridge, just as they were. All four of them turned to face the valley below, where they could see the forest city and the rolling hills and greens laid out in all its splendor. Across the valley floor and beyond the city built in and below the trees, they could see other hills climbing high in the not too far distance, as if the world itself had risen up to nestle the city there in its arms, safe and comfortable.

"We've come from Riverbank Village," Nova said, not quite knowing if she should trust the stranger, but taking her chances and being brave. She wasn't quite sure if she should make known the name of her hometown. She didn't like the idea of calling too much attention to it. Riverbank had long been safe from the outside world, and was separated from the cares of the wider Marchwood. Of course, all of that was changing with each passing day.

"A long voyage, then. Yes, I know those parts. We get our news from the warblers. Do you get the Shennan Gazette your way? We print the most wondrous journals, here. All the news is in them." The great brown bear puffed on his cigar. It smelled not unpleasant, though still a little biting, when it mingled with the fresh air of the waterfalls and the hills. "Strange times, though," he grumbled. "Too much news will make your ears fall off," he joked, and tugged at his left ear.

"Come on, then. I'll walk the way with you. I'm Professor Woodruffe."

"Is there an Academy in Shennan Valley, then?" Nova asked with wonder. She had a great love of books and learning, and had never met a professor.

"Oh, aye, a great one. Though it can't be too great, because they hired me!" Woodruffe laughed heartily and slapped his big belly as he ambled on with the friends down the path. "You know, it's a grand place. That's the thing about an academy; it's the one place where you'll find folks who are after the *truth*. There's a lot of folks and creatures in the world. Some of them want power, some of them want fame, some of them just want to spread their own ideas and indoctrinate others. But when you're in an academy, you know you're mostly surrounded by folks who just want to figure out the *truths* of the world." He took a long draw on the cigar as he walked. "I can't say we're very close to figuring it all out, but we're making progress in the new sciences. Philosophy, on the other hand, well. I can't say that 'progress' is being made in philosophy, of its own accord. I'm still an existentialist, I'd venture, but no one is integrating the discipline of astronomy

169

into the philosophy. We need more communication between the disciplines. But if you want to see a discipline trailing behind the rest of the world, just talk to the philosophers... Well, maybe that's how it should be... philosophy is the slowest of the arts, when you do it right."

The friends nodded their heads and listened attentively. They had never spoken with a professor before. In truth, Woodruffe was on a long and mandatory sabbatical, after a recent publication and surrounding escapade involving a poorly-received treatise on the merits of communal social structures had gotten him some disapproval from his colleagues. While he was at first incensed at the academy's decision to cancel his classes and put him on leave, he decided to "lean into it," as he said, and began referring to the sabbatical as his "most *reverent* and much-needed vacation." Even bears get burned out, after all, and he had grown tired of working through the winter months and lecturing at the top of his lungs in the large lecture halls of the academy, when he should have been hibernating peacefully in his cabin on the outskirts of the city. A much-needed vacation, indeed.

"What's your business in the Shennan Valley, anyway?" Woodruffe asked them.

"Well, it's a bit of a long story," Foxy jumped in. "Perhaps you've heard of the wars in the East. We've had a strange springtime. We intercepted, by chance, a dispatch of a general of Alumbrial, who was going to offer a high price to hire the martens as sellswords to join his war. We've come as ambassadors from Riverbank to seek an alliance with them, instead."

"In fact, we are already growing strong," Klab the toad prince chimed in. "I am prince Klab of Sumbly Swamps, and my toads have joined forces with Riverbank to protect the Marchwood from Alumbrial's invasion. And of course there's this wolf that everyone seems to be talking about, though we know less of his movements and his purpose." The toad croaked importantly.

"Aye, aye, very good, my friends. Though I daresay you might be disappointed to find our leadership is in a mess. The democratic experiment is getting off to a rough start, and everything's grinding to a halt in the Halls of the Grove. The two parties are in a deadlock, you see. The martens and the minks are at loggerheads, and don't even get me started on the gridlock between the contingencies of the weasels and the otters. I doubt you could pass a motion to mend a brick wall, right now, let alone get them to raise an army for you," Woodruffe sighed. "I've heard less about the Wolf of the North, and you know that rumors spread faster than a salmon can jump down a waterfall. I'm inclined to skepticism, but something's brewing that way. We'll have to see."

The words of the professor were comforting to the friends, and they trusted him instantly. He didn't seem to have any pretensions, or any hidden purpose at hand, other than the enjoyment of his long walk, the air itself, and his long, light-wrapped cigar that he loosely between his claws. In short, he seemed an honest fellow, and you can always count on finding good company with folk of that nature.

The four continued ambling down the stone path that lazily crept down the hills and into the valley. They hardly noticed, in the heat of the heavy, breezy June air, that they were descending lower, lower, and lower into the valley floor, and before long they passed through the wooden gate of the Shennan Valley and into the bustling city.

PART THREE

CHAPTER 22

All across Marchwood, the full height of summer was felt through the branch of every tree, on the surface of every leaf, and on the fur of every creature who walked the woods. It was just days, now, before the Summer Solstice, the longest day of the year, and a holiday that was celebrated and known to all the folks of Marchwood. Some called it Midsummer, and some called it Solstice, and some called it Litha, but whatever they called it, it was a time of feasts, friends, sun, peace, and reflection on everything light—and everything dark—in the woods.

Juniper opened her eyes slowly, and felt a stiffness and ache in her head and her body. Still, the warmth of the morning and the gentle angle of the sun encouraged her to open her eyes and look all around her. She was wrapped snugly in a blanket at the foot of a massive, champion basswood tree. Her family had taught her in her youth to label any tree larger than the rest a "champion" of its kind, and this thought always stuck with her. Juniper's memory came back to her, as she thought about her ship, the Waterwheel, and

Admiral Bramblepaw's fleet, and the green-hued storm that rocked their vessels so powerfully and unexpectedly.

When she looked to her left, she saw the leafy undergrowth of the old forest. To her pleasant surprise, when she looked to the right, she was greeted by the warm, worldly smile of a giant red-capped mushroom with an amiable face, wearing a yellow frock and sipping a mug of warm broth. The mushroom was as large as her, and had two very welcoming, very alive, and very blinking eyes, looking lovingly, and right at her.

"You ought to have some. The broth, I mean. I made it for you. Anyway, I'm glad you're awake. My name's Mimsy," the mushroom creature said. "You better take it easy, though. You had quite a tumble." Mimsy had a voice like soft water lapping rocks and wind in evening trees, warm and familiar and melodious.

Juniper rubbed her eyes, wondering if she were dreaming. The pain in her neck and beck as she sat up quickly told her that she was, in fact, wide awake.

"Hello, there," Juniper began. "Have you taken care of me? How very thoughtful," Juniper always remembered her manners, even in this state of general confusion.

"Yes, me and the other Strüm who live here. There are enough of us. Your big friend, the porcupine, has been keeping us busy, though. He's a wily one," Mimsy chuckled.

"The Strüm? Who are the Strüm? Is that what... you are?" Juniper didn't quite know how to ask the question politely, but curiosity inclined her to ask.

"Yes, we are Strüm. Or that's what woodland creatures have called us for years," Mimsy began her explanation. She continued, "We come and go as we please, and don't attach ourselves too much to names. Languages are always growing and changing, just like the forest, and so are names and the folk who are given them. You can call me Mimsy."

"Mimsy? I like that." Juniper listened intently to the mushroom creature.

Mimsy went on, "That's my name for now, yes. In one lifetime, a single Strüm might have as many as a thousand different names, if it makes sense for us to have them, and it often does. Though I suppose I'm getting rather into the thick of it before you've had a chance to wake up. Just call me Mimsy. If you must know, one of the rabbits in your crew described me as an 'upright biped fungus,' and while I'm sure that's mostly accurate, I am not certain it's the best encapsulation of the whole story..."

But Juniper was eager to wake herself and hear the news, whether there was a talking mushroom beside her or not. She stood up, and Mimsy the Strüm offered her arm for support. "Come," said the Strüm, and the two walked around the base of the basswood tree.

There, around the massive trunk, Juniper was sincerely astounded to see hundreds of sailing hares and hundreds of the Strüm folk, eating and chatting and milling about the meadow clearing. She saw the whole of her crew, all safe and sound, and her good friend, Chordy the porcupine. Her ship's crew were having their luncheon on a soft patch of white clover, and honeybees and small white moths flitted about happily around them.

Garnum, the grizzled and long-bearded sailing hare that was aboard Juniper's ship the Waterwheel, was sitting cross-pawed on the grass, as a small Strüm sat on each of his shoulders, chattering away merrily and talking to him. Garnum laughed and told stories, and the Strüm chatted away. Bale the bosun was taking a nap with a Strüm under his head as a pillow, and the Strüm was snoring loudly. One of the mushroom folk on Garnum's shoulder was purple, and the one on the other shoulder was a fiery orange and red. Each Strüm had two deep, black eyes, and they had wide, smiling mouths.

A large yellow Strüm sat on Chordy's belly as he lay in the grasses and clover. It bounced on his belly playfully, as a son or daughter might bounce on a father's tummy, especially after he's overfilled himself at dinner. The calm and serenity of the scene, seeing her friends and her crew all revived and renewed, and peacefully enjoying the morning in the clearing in the woods, calmed all of Juniper's aches and pains and stiffness, and she felt rejuvenated and healed.

Chordy sat up suddenly, sending the yellow-capped Strüm wearing a purple tunic tumbling into the clover. The Strüm bounced and righted herself quickly. They were quick on their feet, these mushroom folk. Chordy looked over and saw Juniper.

"You're all better, then!" Chordy exclaimed excitedly. "We knew you'd get better! The Strüm have healed us all. They're wonderful with wounds and medicines and soups and stories. I don't understand everything they've told me, but I know we owe them more than I can easily say."

Juniper thought her friend Chordy the porcupine sounded clearer and brighter than ever before, and his frame seemed healthy and hale. He had a bandage wrapped around his arm, but otherwise, he looked none the worse for wear. In fact, he looked healthier than ever.

"There's some… magic of the forest, here? Or you have healing powers? You've saved us from the storm?" Juniper asked Mimsy.

"It's not as simple as that, but you're on the right path. Some of your crew called us "magic," but it doesn't mean what you think it does. Sit down and we'll talk with Ralyana, our spore mother."

Mimsy walked Juniper through the clearing over to a large, smooth stone, on top of which sat a wizened and aged Strüm, crinkled and wrinkled but bright in color and sharp of eye, bent over but smiling. This was Ralyana, the spore mother. Sitting next to the Strüm mother was Admiral Bramblepaw of the Riverbank Village fleet, safe and sound.

"Mother, this is one of the captains from the fleet," Mimsy introduced Juniper to the Strüm mother.

Admiral Nilma Bramblepaw jumped down and hugged the young Juniper, and beckoned her to sit down on the log, between Ralyana and herself.

"You've not met our kind before, that I can see," Ralyana spoke slowly, still smiling, and looking over at Juniper. The Strüm mother's eyes showed depth as from another age, another time. There was a glimmer of green and gold flecks deep within the black, as if one might see both the future and the past in their light. "We are only pilgrims in the world. We come and go through the woods, like you. Though we have been here long before and may be here long after, we think. Your crew members have spoken of Mother Elm and the Roots of the World, in the lands where we originate. We can take you there, of course. It's no worry."

"But where are we now?" Juniper asked in wonder.

"Only on the banks of the River Reed at the edge of the Southern Lands," Nilma answered. "The shore is just down the hill, there. Half the crew is busy rebuilding the ships. The sick were taken up here by the mushroom folk after the storm broke. All our fleet has been recovered, except one small vessel, and they're bound to turn up. You took a hit on the head from a swinging boom. A sail unfurled in the high winds. I'm glad you're alright."

Juniper felt the lump on the back of her head, but amazingly, it didn't hurt.

Mimsy clasped her hands together happily. "We mean to go with you, to show you the way down the Great River!"

"The Elm Mother misses you. Every creature of Marchwood should visit the Elm Mother," Ralyana said, slowly.

"You know the Elm Mother, you've seen her?" Juniper's eyes went wide and wider still in astonishment. The old tales and the ancient lore were true, it seemed.

Ralyana the great mushroom mother blinked slowly and her smile widened even further across her cracked and aging but loving face, saying, "All the woods are known through the roots. Every tree speaks to every tree, and every plant to every tree, through the great web that is underneath our feet. Everywhere you walk, there are roots, and water, and voices that speak and listen to one another. We speak to the Elm Mother even now, if we wish, and she listens, and she speaks, and we listen. You only have to know how. Many creatures of the forest have forgotten the way." Ralyana laughed happily, then, and Mimsy smiled knowingly.

Admiral Bramblepaw slapped her knee. "It sounds promising to me, anyway, Juniper. Give it a few days' time and we'll have the fleet in full swing again, and we'll be sailing the River Reed down to the Great River, and we'll meet this Elm Mother and ask for her help."

Juniper hopped off the log and shook paws with the admiral and the Strüm mother Ralyana, followed Mimsy back over to the clearing, and laid down in the clover for a good, long nap. It was nearly the solstice, the longest day of the year, and the sun was not yet risen to its zenith in the sheer blue sky overhead. White towers of smooth, puffy clouds moved steadily like great elephants on a lazy march. The birdsong, and day crickets, and electric buzz of faraway cicadas set Juniper's eyes and ears and mind to sleep.

CHAPTER 23

Nova, Foxy, and prince Klab had already reached the Shennan Valley in the land of the pine martens while Riverbank's leaders were still stuck trying to locate the lost prince and his young friends. The note that prince Klab had left for his father had been misplaced, so the prince was assumed missing, or worse.

As such, the troop that had planned to break west to treat with the pine martens had never left the village at all, and tensions between the toads and the Riverbank villagers grew to a height as supplies were strained and idleness bred trouble. Every day, it seemed, some new brawl had broken out between a group of toad guards and some prejudicial villagers, or some trinket was stolen, or a mug broken, or a sword was drawn in hasty anger.

Search parties that had been sent out into the woods to look for Klab and the two Riverbank Villagers had, of course, turned up nothing, as they were already far off in the rocky pine country of the martens.

Yet, all of these disagreements between Riverbank Villagers and Sumbly Swamp toads became trifles in the minds of all when one day a shrouded figure in a blue and yellow ornate cloak appeared with a band of twenty orderly and polished soldiers carrying tall spears and the banner of a blue-eyed fox. Unannounced and unexpected, they showed up at the gates of Riverbank.

Armored toads readied their bows and villagers with slings stood poised for action on top of the wall walk, looking over the battlements, ready to strike.

The cloaked figure stepped forward. "We come as messengers of Alumbrial the Grave, who now sits on the throne of Goldengrove. These lands are his and his alone. Submit to the rule of Alumbrial's law, and no harm will come to you or your land. If you do not..." the cloaked figure, a tall and slender ferret with oily, brown fur, continued in a sinister tone, "then you will face the swift moving fire of the fury of the fox."

When the bell at had rung at the Meadow Tower to warn of the messenger and his force at the front gate, Father Holbrook had raced down from the archives and climbed the stairs to the battlements. He introduced himself as the representative of Riverbank Village.

Father Holbrook responded to the cloaked figure, "I am Father Holbrook of the Order of the Munks. I speak for my village and for our friends, the toads of Sumbly Swamp. You are welcome to join us in our village to discuss your terms," Father Holbrook called out over the wall, down to the cloaked figure and the armed soldiers. The strange soldiers did look tall and mighty with their long, sharp spears shining in the high sunlight and the pointed peaks on their steel helmets.

The cloaked figure removed the hood from his head. "That's a surprising offer, Father, and one we have not heard before. I accept it."

Krub the Toad King came waddling up the steps, then. He was still in an anxious fury over his missing son, the prince Klab.

"Father Holbrook, you can't possibly imagine letting these ruthless imperialists and usurpers into our village. What if they have some evil intent?" Krub croaked angrily.

"I have some faith in the goodness of the creatures of the Marchwood, still, King Krub. We will see where this leads.

Perhaps Alumbrial's offer will be mutually beneficial. Our design has never been to *wage* war, unless it is needed." Father Holbrook then turned to the guards down by the drawbar of the front gate of Riverbank Village. "Open the gates for our visitors! Open the gates!" Father Holbrook swept his arms in a wide, arcing motion, the sleeves of his robes blowing in the breeze.

The gates of Riverbank Village swung open as the toad guards pushed them, and the mysterious ferret with oily, brown fur walked slowly through the front gate, looking cautiously up at the archers still positioned on the wall walk above him. The score of Alumbrial's heavily armored soldiers with spears, a mix of ferrets and foxes and rats and strong looking wood mice, all marched in unison, following Father Holbrook, who fell in beside their leader and directed them toward the Meadow Tower gathering hall.

Toad guards readied their weapons and Riverbank villagers unsheathed weapons as Alumbrial's soldiers marched through the winding paths of the village. Everywhere there where whispers of the name "Alumbrial" trailing on the breeze. The threat of Alumbrial had always seemed like a distant dream or a fairy tale dragon. Now a score of Alumbrial's soldiers walked their very streets.

"You come from Goldengrove, then? What is your name?" Father Holbrook asked the ferret, as they walked together up the winding stone pathway up the hill toward the Meadow Tower, which they could now see in the distance in the blue-skied day.

"I am Harrmir, agent of Alumbrial. You must excuse me. I am more accustomed to rebuking haughty woodlanders and making *threats* than I am accustomed to being welcomed into villages. Your wisdom and kindness may save you much grief. Many creatures have stood against Alumbrial and fallen, and many yet will. The winds of change burn brightly in the East, and the fires of war will soon reach your hamlet here on the River Reed," Harrmir sighed, dropping from a high, self-important tone to a more casual, friendly manner of speech. "There is peace to be had under strong rule. Alumbrial envisions an empire that would unite the many realms of Marchwood under a single banner and a unified vision of prosperity."

"My dear Harrmir, I'm sure this is a grand vision, but it is well beyond our designs and not in our desires. We are a peaceful folk who have been self-sufficient for centuries. We need no emperor. We need not even a king. We have our gardens and our orchards and our fields and our homes. I'm not sure there is anything you can offer us that would improve our way of life." Father Holbrook smiled as he looked down at the peaceful village of Riverbank over his shoulder. They were now almost at the Meadow Tower on the hill.

As Harrmir and Holbrook and the escort of Alumbrial's soldiers marched up toward the tower, King Krub had other plans. He yelled and cried for every one of his toads to follow him up to the gathering hall, and hundreds of the armored toads swarmed around their leader, donning their helms and capes and shields and tridents and spears. In full force, they were made a small but mighty army—two hundred toads with black capes swirling and the black flag of Sumbly Swamps, forming a line four toads wide, and marching themselves up to the Meadow Tower, not far behind Holbrook and the visitors.

Inside the gathering hall, the circular table that had been used at the Council of War was still laid out. Father Holbrook beckoned Harrmir to sit at the table, and drew a chair for him, and Holbrook sat next to him.

"Well, as much as we enjoy friends and visitors, let's 'cut right into the onion.' What terms does Alumbrial offer? Are they any good?" Father Holbrook chuckled to himself, enjoying his tactic of disarming the mighty Harrmir with kindness. It was often said in Riverbank in those times that "kind words are mightier than swords," and Holbrook meant to test this maxim.

Harrmir was still surprised by what he perceived as Holbrook's impertinence, and could hardly believe that the chipmunk was smiling and laughing. "I'm not sure you understand the gravity of my arrival, Father. Perhaps you are in denial. There is no opportunity for negotiation. Alumbrial sits on the throne of Goldengrove, with an army of twenty thousand. Every town and village, north, south, west, and east of Goldengrove is now kneeling before Alumbrial and entering his service. In return, Alumbrial offers perpetual peace, fair terms, and modest tribute for the maintenance of his empire."

"We heard his army is ten thousand," Father Holbrook prodded. "You wouldn't lie to a munk, would you?"

Harrmir's nose twitched. "His forces grow every day."

"And the Shennan Valley of the pine martens, have they submitted to Alumbrial's rule?" Father Holbrook prodded again.

"Alumbrial's empire grows wide and strong, and many realms are already under the imperial watch." Harrmir's nose twitched again.

"And what laws does Alumbrial propose to keep Marchwood in peace?" Father Holbrook asked.

"His policies are grand, and his rule is just. It is not your place to ask. It is your place to submit to the law of the land." Harrmir grew irate with the chipmunk's questioning.

"In short, you come to our village with false claims, and threaten to harm us if we don't pay tribute and taxes to your emperor, who has no clear plan to rule over us? I am not convinced this is any bargain at all, Harrmir." Father Holbrook leaned forward in his chair and put his elbows on the table. "And I suspect as well that you are aware that you come to us as little more than a bully, as the mouthpiece of one who only pretends to be a great lord, who really has no mind for ruling at all. Your Alumbrial is hungry for power and control, and that is what drives him. I'll say again, we need no emperor. And I'll say more clearly, now, as well, that we decline your offer." Father Holbrook clapped his paws together. "But you are more than welcome to stay for an afternoon meal. I thought a second lunch would do me well, today, and the warm weather is just right for a berry, apple, and walnut salad on some fresh greens. Would you like to join me?"

Harrmir clenched his teeth together, but then relaxed his jaw and shoulders and laughed. "My, you're a cheeky one. I see your meaning. I am only sorry you can't see the wisdom of a unified Marchwood under the great Alumbrial. Well, no matter. My ability to persuade you is irrelevant. But when you see a field of spears and swords and shields and the great machines of war outside your door, you may change your tune, Father." Harrmir sneered.

The Toad King hobbled into the hall. He had been impressed by Father Holbrook's resilience and his method of questioning. "We stand with Riverbank, and so will the pine martens of the Shennan Valley, and many more allies of the

Marchwood will stand with us against Alumbrial. Besides, you will be quite busy with the rogues of the North who are now raising their arms."

Harrmir grew sinister. "The wolf will fall, just as you will." Harrmir threw the hood back over his oily, brown head and signaled to his soldiers that it was time to leave.

Krub motioned to his toad guards, and they escorted the messenger of Alumbrial, and his score of soldiers, out of the gates and back into Marchwood.

Afterward, Krub and Holbrook shook paws and reached an agreement.

"The threat of war is now truly at our doors, Father Holbrook. We must put aside our differences and work together in this. We need no more tension between our soldiers, and no tension between us. I see now there was no plot to kidnap my son, for Nova and the red fox are still missing, as well." The Toad King croaked. "I have been hasty," he admitted.

"I suspect we will hear from them soon enough. I know they must have went off on their own. We shall send more warblers into the skies to seek for them. They must be in the valley of the pine martens by now!" Father Holbrook replied.

Outside the gates of Riverbank Village, Harrmir the agent of Alumbrial took a mental note of the cracked and bowed foundation of the walls, and made a picture in his mind of the treeline that rose so close to the battlements.

CHAPTER 24

The city of Shennan Valley was unlike anything Nova had ever seen. It was built all inside a massive pine forest, and every tree seemed bigger than the next, with deep-lined, ancient bark. Pine needles and pinecones were scattered all across the red brick streets underneath their paws as they walked along the windy roads. Shops, inns, schoolrooms, barracks, armories, hospitals, libraries, and all manner of storefronts and stalls and homes and cabins lined the streets of the city.

Stairs of wood and stone and ladders of rope ascended into the trees, where treehomes were built on branches and platforms and bridges swung from tree to tree and branch to branch. Everywhere hung lanterns on strings that emitted a golden, yellow glow.

A broad, husky looking beaver with a wide, flat tail like a rudder rushed down the street carrying a stack of books in both paws, almost bumping into Nova. A group of otters wearing blue tunics with wool caps were sitting outside an inn, munching on heaping plates of salad and drinking fizzy, yellow, summer drinks with slices of citrus fruit floating around in them. Straight down the middle of the road came a young pine marten mother, pulling a wagon full to the brim with pine marten toddlers, who were tossing balls of blue and gold and silver yarn in the air in a silly, mid-day game of mirth.

Above their heads, weasels and gray squirrels played music on the porch of a treehome. Colorful blankets and clothing set to dry were strung on a line hanging over the railing above. A long-haired squirrel with a kithara strummed and sang while a big, chunky weasel blew on a wide, hardwood bass harmonica. Next to the big, chunky weasel was his sister, who played a thumb piano like a kalimba. Another squirrel was beating on a box drum made from the shell of a massive acorn that had been completely hollowed out. Yet another made bouncing tones on a mouth harp. They played a jaunty folkish ballad that stirred a forlorn feeling in Nova's heart; she thought of home, and hearths, but also of the wider world and the travels she had undertaken. Music has a way of transmitting entire worlds within it, and she thought that this song, coming from above her head from the treehome, perfectly encapsulated the emotion of seeing a new place for the first time, and all the nervous energy and excitement that such an experience could muster.

Professor Woodruffe, the tall, astute, lunking brown bear they had met on the bridge in the rocky heights, nodded his head to the tune, but the music faded as they continued walking through the winding streets. They passed a massive fountain in the shape of a pinecone. There were several large, stone, government buildings, and massive pine trees rose beside and behind them.

"This is the city square," Woodruffe called out. "And over there's the parliament, The Hall of the Groves, or the state house, or whatever they're calling it now. The new government isn't popular. Well, you can hardly call it a government when it does nothing at all, what with the deadlock between the parties," he mumbled, more to himself than to his new companions. "We're about halfway to my home."

The party continued onward, walking beyond the city square with its rows and rows of apartment homes of wood and stone and shops, to a quieter part of the city where the homes became more spaced apart and gardens grew in front and back yards, and tidily trimmed bushes and patches of berries filled in the spaces between the houses.

"This is one of the residential districts, and one of the oldest developments," Woodruffe told them, looking pleased. The bustle of the city gave way to the sounds of warm summer crickets in their mid-day song, and always the electric buzz of some faraway cicada filled in the spaces between the birdsong in the soundscape of the woodland, valley city.

Finally, they turned around a corner of a stone-paved street, walked past a small park with well-born benches, and came upon a one-room, wooden cabin that was tucked far back from the road, and was practically hidden in an overgrown grove of dogwood trees.

"It's called Dogwood House. A simple name for a simple abode. Come on in, you'll like it. I'll get you something to eat," Professor Woodruffe said, proudly. He practically ran to the door, as if he were eager to get home. The roof was a little sloping, and the siding was falling off in places, but the home looked well loved, with a wide, tall, hand-painted sign with too much information on it that read as follows:

- DOGWOOD HOUSE -

- PROFESSOR WOODRUFFE -

- ACADEMY BUSINESS ONLY -

- NO SOLICITING -

- DELIVERIES WELCOME -

- NO KNOCKING BEFORE NOON -

- EXCEPT THE ALE-MAN, KNOCK AT ALL HOURS -

This sign was hanging from the front door, and a wreath of decorative pine branches was underneath it.

Foxy was very curious and felt he had to ask, as he approached the front door, "Who's the Aleman?"

"You don't have an *ale*-man in Riverbank Village? They bring the ale, right to your front door! Better than a *mail*-man. No one wants mail; it's all bills and advertisements. One hardly receives a good letter anymore, these days," Woodruffe chuckled from the bottom of his belly. "Of course, it's not proper to say ale-man any longer. It's often an ale-beaver, otter, mouse, skunk, or a stoat, girl or boy. Anyone and everyone is welcome to deliver ale to *my* front door!"

Professor Woodruffe laughed heartily, as if the very thought of big crates of ale delivered to the front door was enough to make life worth living itself, and the very happiness of his soul seemed to erupt with the laughter from his belly.

Inside the cabin was nothing out of the ordinary, which pleased his new friends, who were more than a little worn from their long and unexpected journey. Dogwood House was simple, clean, swept, and minimal. An iron cookstove was the centerpiece of the home, and there were a few pieces of sparse, wooden furniture: a table, three chairs, two stools that didn't match, a patterned red and blue rug with stitchwork depicting trees and castles and some history of old wars, and an assortment of bookshelves, some low, and some so high they reached the ceiling. Light came into the cabin from the front bay window and from smaller, geometric windows on the side walls facing east and west. The ceiling had a large skylight window that faced to the south, and the light danced into the cabin from the skylight after passing through the leaves of the dogwood trees that canopied the home.

"Your home is very cozy, Professor Woodruffe," Nova said. "It reminds me of my tiny stone home in Riverbank."

"Thank you, thank you. It's one of the first cabins built in the valley. She's an old dwelling, but tough. And you can nearly smell the history of it," the bear took in a big sniff. "Doctor Norgruff Barrelbarrow built it with his own two paws, more than two centuries ago. He was one of the founding members of the Shennan Academy. I'd like to buy the cabin from the Academy Trust, but they don't often part with their real estate assets..." Woodruffe trailed off. "Do you like coffee? I drink it black and oily but I could put some honey and sugar in it if you wanted. Black's the way a bear drinks coffee. That's how it's done in the valley."

"We'll do it your way! Black and... oily," Nova smiled politely.

Woodruffe poured out mugs of the thick, black coffee, and waved his paws to offer the friends a seat at the table in his small but comfortable cabin. He cracked opened the windows and a warm breeze blew in through the dogwoods, and Nova felt almost right at home, as if she were sitting with a mug of Valerian tea in Riverbank Village, and Foxy was reminded of simpler times in the fox den of his youth.

CHAPTER 25

South of Riverbank Village, Juniper and her crew were mending their ships and healing their bodies after the battering of the green storm that had rocked their boats and scattered the fleet. Countless Strüm had run out from the woods and rescued the rabbits as they washed up on shore in the thundering downpour. In the storm, the Strüm climbed aboard the vessels and anchored them to the shore, carried unconscious hares up into the safety of the canopy of the woods, and set to making their potions—*pharmakon,* they called them—with the plant medicines of the forest.

The rabbits at first took to describing the mushroom folk as "upright, biped fungi," but it was soon found to be an altogether insufficient description. They were, in fact, magic creatures of the woods who knew great truths about the nature of the world, and could speak with the trees through the vast network of fungal roots that connected every elm and oak, every sapling to its mother, every flower to its father, every bush and every turnip and every fern.

Juniper the red rabbit and Mimsy the Strüm became fast friends. Other Strüm, especially the curious Strüm children, enjoyed climbing onto the backs and shoulders of the rabbits and nestling in between the ears on tops of their heads.

"We'll depart the day after the Summer Solstice," Admiral Bramblepaw announced that day. "Our ships are ready and our friends are true. We owe every thanks to these gentle creatures of the woods. And they have agreed to show us the way to the Great River to find the paths to the Elm Mother." A great cheer went up in the peaceful clearing in the woods where the hares and Strüm had made a temporary camp to nurse their wounds while repairs were ongoing with their fleet.

The departure was set for the day after the Summer Solstice, for both the Strüm and the Riverbank hares had long celebrated the seasonal holiday and longest day of the year. While the Strüm called this special day *Litha*, the hares were likely to call it Midsummer Eve and Midsummer, or just The Solstice.

The two races of creatures shared their traditions in the clearing where they made their temporary camp. The hares, for their part, carried large wooden chests and rolled big barrels of supplies from their galleys, and brought tables and chairs up from below deck and into the woods. They had made their camp just a short walk up from the shore, where the fleet of rabbit vessels were now safely anchored in the warmth of the June days. There had been some rain, again, after the heavy storm that nearly sunk their fleet, but it was nothing too serious. It was mostly light drizzles and warm showers that led to more dancing than fretting.

By the time the day of the Solstice celebration arrived, the ships had all been repaired, and the clearing had been transformed into a festival setting that was ready for a feast of grand proportions. The Strüm were expert craftmakers, and made garlands of flowers to hang around the necks of their new friends, the rabbits of Riverbank Village. The Strüm also showed the hares how to play the stalkflute, a simple instrument made from knotweed, a bamboo-like plant that grew invasively in Marchwood. The Strüm had grown frustrated in trying to rid the Marchwood of this invasive species, and so decided to make use of it instead, creating several different instruments from its hollow stalk, including pan flutes, stalkflutes, and a sort of giant, knotweed marimba made from different lengths of hardened stalks of the plant.

The Strüm crafted curious and extraordinary bouquets from every species of plant in the woods. They could twist leaves and grasses into twirling bows and find the perfect blends and hues of matching petals and wildflowers to weave together into fresh displays of sweet smelling, eye pleasing arrangements, which they placed on every table and trestle that had been set up in the meadow clearing. On the trestle tables, the Strüm heaped massive bowls and platters filled with edible plants of the woods: red and white and orange and purple tubers, bundles of sweet and spicy roots, salads of intricate greens and purples, teas made from dandelion and burdock and chamomile, and enchanting brews like their rosemary wine and spring daisy cordial and rose hip spirits.

Tower over all their heads and in the very center of the clearing was a creation of the hares: a tall, wooden structure made from sticks and twigs and fallen, gathered burning material. The mass of sticks and fallen limbs and logs and twigs had been shaped into the figure of a big, plump hare with two towering ears. All around this effigy—for the giant hare made of wood was to be burned on the longest day of the year as the sun set—there were placed wheels made of bent and twisted wood and dead plant matter.

The wheels were the contribution of the Strüm, who viewed the Solstice not only as a day of celebration but as a time of reflection on the battle between the primary forces of the woods: life and death, or light and dark, or being and nothingness. The Strüm believed that on this day, the force of life gave way to the force of death, but they accepted this passing of power from one hand to the next. As Ralyana, the elder Strüm mother explained to Juniper, "Without nothingness, there is no being from which to contrast ourselves, strange as that may seem. Without death, there is no life. Without dark, there is no light. We remember this in every waking moment, for every evening gives way to night's shining stars, and every night gives way to every morning's dawn, and every dawn to the afternoon..."

Juniper and Mimsy kept themselves busy by swapping stories about their friends and families.

"I'd like to visit Riverbank Village after we return from the Elm Mother. Do you think some of the Strüm would be welcome there?" Mimsy asked her new friend.

"I'm certain of it," Juniper replied happily. "Our gates are always open to peace-loving creatures, and you would fit right in. And I'm sure that Father Holbrook and Mother Glamdrill, and many of our sages and munks—chipmunks that is—and all the other folk who live there would be pleased to meet you. We have much to learn, I'm sure, of where you come from and what you know. I've never heard of your folk, and we have no records in our libraries of the Strüm."

"You've been living under a rock!" Mimsy joked.

"Maybe not a rock, but behind our walls, yes. We haven't ventured out beyond our walls like this in years and years," Juniper told her.

As the longest day of the year arrived, the hares presented gifts to Ralyana and the Strüm folk in a casual but sincere ceremony in the center of the clearing, before the feast began. Strüm and hares worked together to set the tables with every manner of fare, from the heaping plates of salads and berries and fruits to edible garnishes—tiny bouquets of fresh herbs and grasses—and main courses of baked carrots with honey glaze, thick soups of tomato and basil, and wild yellow and red and green sweet peppers filled with a rich, salty, savory bread stuffing with rock salt and oil from the hare's larders.

Finally, the feast began, and Strüm and rabbit ate, laughed, and loved the day, as bellies were filled and hearts were warmed with the good food, good friendship, and sweet musical tones of the stalkflutes that every sailor now knew how to play and many kept strung about their neck by hemp string.

Juniper took a big bite of one of the stuffed sweet peppers with the bread filling, crumbs falling down onto her lap. "I should hardly like to leave, *mmph* this is good!" She said to her friend Mimsy, the Strüm.

Mimsy crunched on the fresh purple and greens of a big plate of salad, using her hands to eat one leaf at a time and savoring every bite. "We're always leaving, and going. You know what my mother said? You can never step on the same blade of grass twice. By the time you return, it has grown and changed into a different blade altogether. Every day is different and everything is always in movement and motion, subtle and vibrating. Lovely isn't it?" Mimsy mumched.

"The motion of everything? Yes, it is lovely, I think. Though I was never much of a philosopher. I'm starting to see how the world looks from your perspective, Mimsy."

"No, no, I meant the salad is lovely! But *that*, too!" Mimsy laughed.

By the end of the feast, the evening was turning to night, and the dark blue dragonflies of the evening flew overhead as Ralyana and Admiral Bramblepaw each walked solemnly up to the giant bonfire effigy in the center of the clearing, and dropped their torches to the base of the wood structure.

The creatures formed a great circle around the tower to watch as the flames started low and quickly burst upward through the sticks and twigs and wood of the rabbit-shaped bonfire, and a jarring but happy *crack-crackle!-crack-crack-crackle!* sounded sweetly through the calm, warm, darkening night.

Moths gray and white and black made circles around the fire, as finally the very top of the tower, the rabbit ears, went up in a powerful *whoosh!* and there was cheering among the crowds, and music played on through the night.

CHAPTER 26

"You may have noticed the city is quite busy," Woodruffe told Nova, Foxy, and Klab. "Well, it's always busy," he grumbled, but then continued, "but it's almost the Solstice, I'm sure you know. So things are busier than usual. And there is always the Solstice Festival this time of year. The Hall of Groves, the parliament, that is, won't even be in session for another week. You're best to just enjoy the season and the festivities," He sipped his coffee thoughtfully. "Though I appreciate your aplomb. I like your style. I'll help you every way I can."

The thick, black, oily coffee had excited the nerves of Nova and Foxy. The brew seemed to have no effect on Klab, the toad prince, who was accustomed to drinking large amounts of mashes and grogs in the black castle of the swamps. From the effects of Professor Woodruffe's coffee, Nova and Foxy had fallen into relaying the entirety of their story to the bear in the tweed jacket and wool cap.

The professor lit a long, fresh cigar and listened attentively. The open windows carried away the smoke in blue, wispy tendrils. Fresh air filled in from the angular, many-sided windows of the warm, late June day. Everywhere was the inescapable but hearty and comforting scent of pine. Pine wood and pine trees and pine sap composed the prevailing odor of the entire city—which was much better than many cities, which can easily smell of soot and industry and rotten things if they are not well tended. While the pine tree city of the Shennan Valley was not perfect—as nothing is perfect—it certainly had been well tended through the years.

"We'd never heard of Alumbrial before," Nova leaned her elbows on the table as she recounted the events of the spring to the professor. "And so we made a treaty with the toad king —as you know, this is his son, the prince Klab. But the expedition was taking too long, so we left ahead of them. We haven't heard any word."

"We should send a note by warbler. You're likely missed at home. Does Riverbank receive warblergrams? There's a network of warblers that send messages all throughout Marchwood. I suppose you've heard of it?"

They nodded—while Riverbank wasn't on a main message route, there was a small warbler station in Riverbank which could receive messages, but it got more use by those birds who needed to rest while they were making longer flyovers.

"We ought to send a message back so they aren't wondering about us. I did think it was strange that Grubbels and his troops didn't catch up to us. I hope there's no trouble back at home. Maybe Alumbrial is moving faster than we thought," Foxy said.

"As far as Alumbrial goes, the news is not great," Professor Woodruffe admitted, and he pulled a rolled-up newspaper out from a shelf just behind him. "Look, here. The headline says, 'GOLDENGROVE FALLS TO SELF-DECLARED EMPEROR ALUMBRIAL.' There's quite a bit more. Foxes and rabbits and mice displaced, mass migrations, homes destroyed, fires, usurpation. Some creatures are resisting, it seems... the Blue Foxes in the Snowhills, for one example... It's ill news, there's no question about it. But it's not hopeless. After all, he doesn't seem to have much of a policy or vision in the grand scheme of things, not that I can tell. Marchwood can unite against Alumbrial. You know, it would be one thing if we were uniting under a well-defined common purpose, but this business of Alumbrial is just the greed of a tyrant." Professor Woodruffe handed the pulpy newspaper over to Nova. The blueberry ink stained her hands as she shuffled it around and read it. She had never held a newspaper before.

"What about you, professor? Are you worried about the Shennan Valley? Will Alumbrial reach you here?" Nova asked, looking over at her friends, Foxy and Klab. She passed the newspaper over to Foxy, but he didn't read it. It was still too raw in his memory, having escaped from the very events that were there described in the blue ink.

"I couldn't tell you, dear. My ways are mostly unaffected by the bigger going-ons. I'm more of a thinking bear..." The ash of his cigar fell on his leg and he suddenly let out a growl and brushed it off. "No, I tell you, though. I'd like to get involved. That's why I'm going to help you. I've had my head in the books for a little too long. Not that there's anything wrong with that, someone has to try to figure out why we're here and how we should conduct ourselves. The world's a mess. But what's needed right now is action, and I'm going to help you." The bear smiled, and put his massive paw across the table.

Foxy, Nova, and Klab all put their paws on top of Woodruffe's.

"But first," the bear said, "I think we have a little bit of time to join in the fun. Here's the plan. I know my district's representative—we're sort of a municipal republic—and I can bring you to him in the Hall of the Groves after the Solstice celebrations are concluded. We'll make our petition to him, and we'll see what he thinks about raising an army to help Riverbank. At the least, we'll get his feedback and suggestions. And the best outcome is we might be able to forge an alliance that will help keep our two lands in peace, together. Are you willing to fight a bit for it? I don't know that it'll be easy."

"We're ready," Nova said. "We'd do anything to save our home."

"Alright, well. First things first. Let's get off to the Warbler Station to send off a message to Riverbank. We'll make sure they're updated," Professor Woodruffe decided.

The four of them left the cabin, their minds excited by the coffee, and walked quickly down the stone pathways that connected every street and corridor of the pine tree city of Shennan Valley. The Warbler Station was a rickety old shack tucked away just a few streets down the way, next to a potion shop. Nova thought she saw a big, walking mushroom through the window of the potion shop nextdoor, but she blinked her eyes and thought perhaps it was just the coffee working its way on her.

Inside the Warbler Station was a gray hare with a long mustache and thin, scraggly beard. He wore a white and blue tunic and a ragged cap with a visor.

"Howdy, professor! What are we sending off today? Is it another manuscript? I've got a big, fat russet-crowned warbler that could carry a sack of potatoes a hundred miles if you needed 'em to. Who are your friends?" The gray hare had yellowed teeth but smiled pleasantly with them.

"Howdy Jams, how's business? These are my friends from Riverbank. We need to send a message back home. Got a scrap of paper?" Woodruffe asked.

"Sure, sure. Riverbank, 'eh? Not too far. I've got a little wren that's itching for a flight. She could probably handle it today. Weather's fine, a little hot, though," Jams the gray hare said. Behind the counter of the Warbler Station shop, and behind Jams's head, there were twenty or thirty songbirds twittering and jumping and hopping on branches and shelves, some of them pecking at nuts and birdseed, some with messages tied to their legs, others wearing tiny backpacks with scrolls stuffed in them.

"Funny, Juniper was telling me all about warblers just this spring. I don't know one from another," Nova remembered.

Professor Woodruffe looked over at the three friends. "What should we say?" He picked up the pen and started to scribble on the note paper. "Maybe something like: *Arrived.* Full stop. *Negotiations pending.* Full stop. *Will report more, one week.* Full stop. *N. F. K.* How does that sound? I got that right, hey? Nova, Foxy, Klab? N. F. K." The big bear chuckled. "There's an art to writing short messages. The birds can't carry much. Is that alright?"

The three nodded. Nova said, "That sounds very fine and official, I think. Can you add 'Happy Solstice'? Make sure it's addressed to Father Holbrook. He'll be able to spread the message to Grubbels and King Krub and the others. How long will it take for the message to arrive? Is it expensive?"

Jams the gray hare leaned over on the counter. "I'll send it with my fresh little yellow-crested warbler, here, no worries. It won't take more than a few days for her to get over that way, as the warbler flies. We run a tight service, here. They might even send something back to you. Should I charge it to your account, professor?" The gray hare suddenly narrowed his eyes. "You've got a bit of a balance…"

"*Ahem*. Excuse me. Yes, please charge it to the account. I'll get around to it, no worries. I haven't got my pocketbook on me today. Been a bit of an unusual summer, you know." He looked a bit flustered, but in fact the balance was not very high for a bear of his means and the professor had indeed forgotten his pocketbook at home, in the drawer where he usually left it.

Jams delicately wrapped the message to the wren's leg, walked over to the back of the shop, opened a tiny circular window in the low ceiling, and the wren flew off into the blue sky.

On the days leading up to the Solstice, the city of the Shennan Valley was bedecked with garlands and wreaths and lanterns and bonfires, as bands of troubadours marched down the street with banners and in swelling, merry processions.

Finally, on the day of the Solstice itself, there was the famous midnight parade that wound its way all through the city, and in which the inhabitants of the valley all participated. The parade began at eleven o' clock at the front gate of the city, and circled around the streets in a swirling pattern until thousands of creatures in costumes and armors and festive attire met in the city square at the giant pinecone fountain.

In the excitement of the dark of night, Nova, Foxy, and Klab fell right into the parade with the honest bear, Professor Woodruffe, who had fast become a good friend to them. A big beaver father with a bushy, wiry beard and a long, wide tail in a floppy yellow hat was marching alongside of them, blowing on a brass horn, and wearing nearly ten big, sunflower garland necklaces around his neck. Everywhere was the sound of drums and horns and pennywhistles in the nighttime parade procession. The warm, orange and yellow glow of lanterns and bonfires in steel drums and stone firepits offered some light onto the streets and their faces. The beaver came closer to the four.

"You're not dressed the part! You must not be from around here! Oh, hello Professor!" The beaver smiled, and immediately started taking the sunflower garlands from around his neck and handing them to the friends. "You've got to wear these! We're saying goodbye and hello at the same time!" The beaver was shouting over the din and excitement of the parade procession. "We say goodbye to the spring and hello to the summer!" The beaver yelled to them, smiling all the while.

"Or goodbye to the light and hello to the dark, in the old ways," Professor Woodruffe yelled back. His baritone voice boomed out over the celebratory cacophony of sounds.

"No, no, that's too depressing, professor! I like to say 'Hello, summer!' Winter's a long way away. It's bad luck to even talk about the winter on the Solstice! You might upset the trees." The Beaver was laughing and ran off down the street between crowds and crowds of creatures, handing out sunflower garlands and tiny brass horns as he went.

As the parade procession with its bands of drummers and musicians and otters and beavers blowing horns and waving banners and handkerchiefs all about in the air made its way to the city square, Professor Woodruffe found a comfortable spot near the edge of the crowd, and lifted the three friends up onto a high, brick wall around a garden bed in front of a large stone building.

"You're in for a treat. We've got a great display of fireworks this year. It's the talk of the town. A wizard mouse named

Míomar wandered into town, just a few days ago, with a great wagon full of the finest fireworks anyone's ever seen."

"A wizard? Fireworks?" Nova asked, wonder in her voice. These were unfamiliar words in Riverbank Village, though distant memories seemed to flash in her mind of a story her father had told her when she was just a tiny squirrel kit.

"His arrival was completely unexpected, as you might expect of a wizard," Professor Woodruffe laughed. "Some say that wizards bring storms with them, which may be true..." He tilted his head back up at the sky, looking about the tops of the towers and buildings at the stars above, and the great swirl of the galaxy, "but that's only because they come just when they're needed. The storm brews first, and we're lucky they pay attention. Always listen to a wizard," he said.

Just as Professor Woodruffe finished his musings, and the friends swung their legs out over the ledge and got to sitting comfortably, a sizzling, soaring rocket shot up straight in the sky from a platform on top of the Hall of Groves, leaving a trail of burning bright orange light through the sky. Then *boooom!* the rocket cracked apart, and a blue and yellow flower of sparks and shining light exploded in the air above the city square, flashing and shining colored light over the face of every otter, weasel, stoat, bear, squirrel, fox, and beaver in the city. Again, a sizzling, soaring sound roared through the warm, midnight air and two more fireworks flew up into the sky, and *craaaack!* they went, popping and sizzling and booming in silvers and golds, dark greens and bright greens, reds and oranges.

Pop! pop! pop! they went, one after another. *Pop! pop!* Some took the shape of the crescent moon, and others like ripe red berries on the vine, and some just like sparkling circles in rows and bunches, and Klab's favorite was one with pink and silver sparks in the shape of flower petals floating downward on a breeze, rocking back and forth in a gentle motion, cascading and raining downward slowly and serenely.

At last, a sound like a gale blew through the square all of a sudden, and a wide tower of a rocket shot up into the sky, higher than the others. As it *boomed!* over their heads, it mushroomed upward even higher into the shape of a worldly trunk, with a thousand spiraling branches, making a canopy of golden yellow leaves. The sizzling, fizzing sparks stayed in the sky for longer than anyone could imagine possible, and to the surprise of all—for they thought that this was the grand finale and last of the ó's fireworks—a small, narrow rocket shot up into the sky, and *crack!* it went in a small burst, and the sparks grew into a long, thin, bright green sapling with small branches and leaves in every direction, next to the much larger tree.

"The big tree is meant to represent Mother Elm, I think. And the little one is... a sapling, perhaps. A sapling," the professor thought to himself, feeling clever at understanding the portent.

Foxy put his hands in his pockets and tilted his head back, grinning from ear to ear. He looked over at Klab, and they nodded in approval at one another, and he looked over at Nova, who was transfixed, staring straight up at the sky.

"What a night!" Foxy said, to himself, but the others heard him clearly and nodded their heads up and down in agreement. "What a night!"

Before they left the city square, Professor Woodruffe led his new friends to a small stall on a side-street, just away from the square. An old mother pine marten was tending the stall, and she had three large baskets of curious, plump looking fruits.

Professor Woodruffe picked one up and showed Nova, Foxy, and Klab. "This is a scarlet plum. Have you ever had one?"

They had never seen the small, palm-fitting, dark red fruit, but as soon as Nova bit into the plump, juicy skin, warmed by the day, she fell in love with the not-too-sweet, not entirely sour, ripe, red scarlet plum. The red juices trickled down her chin fur as she ate the first, and filled all the happy places in her mouth, underneath and on the sides of her tongue.

"It's perfect," Nova said, through her bites. Foxy and Klab bit into the scarlet plums merrily.

"Just don't eat one on a first date. You'll make a mess, stain your fur," Professor Woodruffe chuckled.

"Here, have a few for the road," the old pine marten mother said to them, and handed out a few more. "It's the Solstice, after all."

Professor Woodruffe winked at the old pine marten, and smiled. She was a dear friend of his and a nearby neighbor in his part of the city.

"Now, mind you don't eat the pit in the middle, and don't choke on it. But put that pit in your pocket and when you get back home you can plant it and grow your own scarlet plums in Riverbank Village. Wouldn't that be swell?"

They all saved the pits in their pockets, and when they returned to Dogwood House, they slept peacefully through the night with blankets and pillows on the cool wood floor of the home, with the faraway sounds of revelry and celebrations and horns and music leaving them feeling satisfied and happy with the world.

CHAPTER 27

In Riverbank Village, preparations for the Summer Meadowfest were well underway. Tensions had been resolved between Father Holbrook and the Toad King, and spirits were high again, as the newfound friendship between Riverbank villagers and the toads of Sumbly Swamp had been solidified. Friendship prevailed, and the brawling subsided, as the toads and villagers became not only accustomed to each other but fast friends and faithful allies, feeling full well the strengthening of their bond under the threat of Alumbrial's invasion. Nothing so strengthens the bond between folks as a common goal—in this case, as well, a common enemy.

Bargles, the armored guard of the Toad King, showed his friend Rudbeck the mouse how to prepare a cattail crown. In toadish tradition, the cattail crown was worn on Midsummer's Day to help ward off the forest spirits who would seek to shorten the days. The toads would then play competitive games with blunt spears—wooden poles, really—to try to knock the crowns from the other's head.

Smacking your opponent was entirely against the rules, and would disqualify a combatant. You could only knock the crown off the other's head. Nonetheless, the game became incredibly competitive, as toads could knock their sticks together to try to throw off their opponent, and use their stick to block swings. Occasionally, a skilled entrant could even disarm an opponent (which would not necessitate a victory, but often would).

Rudbeck had helped the toads carry big stones up from the banks of the River Reed to make a large stone circle on the flat ground behind the Meadow Tower on the hill. The stone circle would make the sparring ground for the toad's game, which they simply called "King of the Ring." The winner of the brackets would get to wear the Iron Crown of the Toad King for the entirety of the day of the Solstice, and could make one petition to the king—that is, the winner could make one request, and the Toad King would consider it, and usually grant it, if it was a fair and reasonable request.

Bargles helped Rudbeck train in a practice session the morning of the event.

"No, you've got to keep your stick up. It's a bit like swordplay, but remember they're trying to swing *over* your head, not at it," Bargles coached. They were practicing down by the river bank the morning of the Solstice—or Midsummer —as the sun grew higher in the sky on the longest day of the year. At noon, when the sun was the highest in the sky it would be all year, is when the competition would start in the ring of stones.

Rudbeck wiped the sweat off his ears, and lifted his fighting pole high.

"Keep it at an angle," Bargles called, and smacked out with his stick. The sting from the hard hit nearly numbed Rudbeck's paws to the bones, and he felt the vibrations up through his elbow.

But Rudbeck showed plenty of promise in his skill at the game, as he was more precise and nimble than the toads. Toads are fast hoppers and can move in a single direction with great speed, but they are not often artists with their weapons, which is why they prefer the spear and shield to the complex combat of swordplay.

Rudbeck, on the other hand, had taken combat lessons with Captain Grubbels as a child, as the two mice had formed a bond when Rudbeck was a babe, and Grubbels had taken in Rudbeck like a grandson. Grubbels was at first disappointed that his young protege had decided not to enlist under his regiment, but, in a sense, was proud in part of Rudbeck's rebellious nature and free-thinking spirit. After Rudbeck had dropped out of Grubbels's regiment, the old veteran mouse had told him, "There are a thousand paths through life. You need not follow mine precisely, even if you walk at times in my footsteps." These were comforting words for Rudbeck, who respected and loved the old mouse.

Slap! went Bargles with his rod, and Rudbeck's crown of cattails went flying off his head and broke in two.

"Hey, I wasn't paying attention," Rudbeck grumbled, picking up the crown and trying to weave it back together, as Bargles had taught him.

"Exactly," Bargles laughed. "You weren't paying attention."

But at noon, when scores of armored toads and scores of Riverbank villagers gathered around outside the Meadow Tower to watch as the games commenced, Rudbeck found himself winning battle after battle as he deftly knocked the cattail crowns from his opponents' heads. He ducked, bobbed, and weaved and invented his own style of mastering the game that took the toads by surprise.

Villagers waving handkerchiefs and drinking cool, bubbly drinks from copper and wooden mugs crowded around and cheered Rudbeck on.

King Krub and Father Holbrook stood right at the edge of the stone circle, among the crowd, doing their own cheering and shouting.

"Come on, Rudbeck! You can do it!" Father Holbrook cheered out, his hands clasped excitedly around his mouth. The toads and villagers loved seeing the sagely chipmunk getting into the spirit of the games. Even Captain Grubbels had called off drills for the festivities of the Solstice, and stood with his hands on his hips enjoying every match, his mustache twitching as he watched.

Beyond the massive circle of the spectators, trestle tables had been laid out in the summer sun with every manner of woodland treat for the high noon Solstice luncheon. There were countless casks of Chef Goodknee's heavy, hearty, bubbling Riverbank Stout of Heart brew, which was now the favorite drink of nearly every woodlander who lived in Riverbank Village. Piles of fresh, smoked almonds with seasoning, massive bowls of spinach and red onion and cucumber salads, and trays of blueberries and raspberries and blackberries lined every table. There were platters of honey-baked crunchy granola and savory pies and sweet pies and red and orange sunberry tarts.

Chef Goodknee had also revealed his new, signature dish to mark the festive occasion of Midsummer meal: thick slices of plump, juicy, sun-kissed peaches arranged atop a fresh, creamy, sugary whipped base that was dense and sweet. "The Yellow Meadow," he named it, simply, and it was already becoming a new favorite of the villagers and toads alike.

Rudbeck worked his way through the ranks all day, as the high sun moved through the afternoon, and finally, a few clouds dulled the rays, and a breeze blew in from the west. Rudbeck won the top spot in his bracket and a chance to be claimed King of the Ring if he could win the championship match.

The final duel was against a hulking, tall toad by the name of Imbruk, who wore a long, black cape and the full armor of the toad guards.

Imbruk was not the most skillful competitor, but his massive size made the cattail crown on top of his head difficult to knock off. Paired with his long reach and gargantuan strength, Imbruk had swept through the matches of his bracket with ease.

"Two worlds meet in the heat of the sun, my friend!" He bellowed out at Rudbeck the mouse. Imbruk never underestimated his opponents, and had heard how the mouse had become a clever and crafty competitor. They shook paws, and Imbruk took one last swig of his Stout of Heart brew before the match was underway.

King Krub waved the black flag of battle, and shouted, "Begin!"

To Rudbeck's advantage, the hulking Imbruk had feasted heavily throughout the games, and was slowed by the food and the drink. But with his thick arms he could smash out with his rod with dangerous force, and he had disarmed more than one of his opponents that very day.

Imbruk started powerfully with a sideways blow, hoping that Rudbeck would attempt to block the fearsome swing. But Rudbeck side-stepped and ducked under the swing, coming up on Imbruk's right side. Imbruk grasped his rod in two hands and blocked Rudbeck's counter attack, then pushed out forcefully, knocking Rudbeck back, and the mouse stumbled.

In that moment of stumbling, Imbruk paced forward and beat out left and right with his pole, hoping to make the mouse walk backward and stumble out of the ring for an easy win.

Rudbeck rose to the challenge, and ducked again under Imbruk's blows, coming up behind him. With a quick upward thrust and prod of his pole, Rudbeck knocked the cattail crown from Imbruk's head!

It was all over in an instant, and an extraordinary roar went up from the villagers—and many toads, who had cheered on the newcomer—and hats and caps and handkerchiefs were thrown into the air in celebration.

King Krub croaked happily, seeing the gain in a Riverbank villager winning the competition, and the humility and wisdom it would bring on his guards.

"Rudbeck is King of the Ring!" Krub, King of Toads shouted, and all throughout the grounds behind the Meadow Tower, there were shouts of "Rudbeck! Rudbeck! King of the Ring! King of the Ring!"

Rudbeck shook paws with Imbruk, who was still very much trying to piece together how he had lost the match.

Imbruk laughed, then, and bellowed out over the din, "Cheers to the young mouse, Rudbeck the Bold!" and new cries of "Rudbeck the Bold! Rudbeck the Bold!" rang out through the crowd and into the afternoon sun. Imbruk lifted up Rudbeck the mouse onto his shoulders and paraded him through the cheering crowds, and Rudbeck lifted his arms high over his head.

When the cheering died down, Imbruk set Rudbeck back down in the middle of the circle of stones, and the Toad King, Krub, hopped over to him. Everyone grew silent and watched on in anticipation. The King of the Ring was always granted one petition to King Krub, but an outsider had never before won the title.

"My honorable friend, Rudbeck the Bold," the Toad King began, "I present to you the Iron Crown, which you shall wear through Midsummer, to remind us all of the wisdom found in friends, and to teach us the love of our neighbors. You may present to me today, before midnight, a single petition, which I will consider with earnest heart and the full concentration of my spirit."

The Toad King removed the Iron Crown from his head, and removed the cattail crown from Rudbeck. Then, the Toad King placed the Iron Crown on Rudbeck's head, and the cattail crown on his own.

"The King of Midsummer has been crowned," Krub proclaimed, holding aloft Rudbeck's paw. "Now let the feasts begin in earnest, and we will bring in the Solstice together, as allies, and, more importantly, as friends!"

EPILOGUE

The feasting and frolicking and merry-making continued all through the Solstice Day, and then into the dusk, and into the night, as the stars came out over Marchwood. Even in the days after, songs were sung, and new songs were written by woodland creatures sitting next to campfires and bonfires and in trees and under trees, and new friends were made and old friends rediscovered. Creatures everywhere ate and drank and sang and celebrated, from the Southern streams of the River Reed where Juniper danced in the moonlight by the great bonfire in the clearing, to the pine forests of the West where Nova, Foxy, and Klab reveled in the great woodland city of Shennan Valley, to the quiet village of Riverbank where villagers danced the Summer Three-step in the lantern-lit tents with friendly toads.

But in the East, the inhabitants of the towering capital city of Goldengrove celebrated privately in their homes, as the heavily armed soldiers of Alumbrial's army patrolled the streets and kept a strict curfew. Families of foxes and otters and mice shut their windows and locked their doors, and most families read books or left the city altogether, hauling wagons of their belongings to seek new settlements in new plains. Marchwood had never seen an emperor—and all knew they had no need for one—and the fast-moving forces of Alumbrial the Grave had taken the entire city and its surrounding settlements by surprise. Everywhere in the East, roads were crowded with refugees, regiments of soldiers on the move, and patrols of messengers that had been sent all over the Marchwood.

One such messenger was Harrmir, the tall and slender ferret with oily brown fur in a regal cloak who had visited Riverbank Village with commands from Alumbrial the Grave. After his visit with Father Holbrook, Harrmir sincerely doubted his alignment with Alumbrial's cause.

"Perhaps the villagers are right. What business does an emperor have in a self-sufficient riverside village of peaceful chipmunks and squirrels?" He muttered to himself as he walked along the crowded Great Road back to Goldengrove, a score of the spear-soldiers following behind him. "I should have brought a companion on the road to talk with. Bounce some ideas around. Maybe that was Alumbrial's design. He wants to leave us to our tortured thoughts, out on the road," he went on to himself. "Then again, an empire will protect sleepy villages like Riverbank. This rogue wolf from the North, for one, could come down at any time and sack such a village in an instant. They should be thankful for our offer," Harrmir puffed.

From the tallest tower of the city of Goldengrove, Alumbrial the Grave, who was in truth a fox of middling height who wore platform boots to make himself appear taller, leaned out of a stone windowsill in the room he had taken up as a temporary command post. The sun was setting, and he imagined himself as ruler of all that he surveyed with his eyes. What he did not realize, of course—because he then lacked the wisdom—was the fleeting nature of power, and the misfortune and misery that his abrupt seizure of Goldengrove had caused in the city. He imagined all of his decisions were graced by the light of the sun and the moon, and that he could do no wrong.

But as the dark grew deep in the early hours of Midsummer's night, far in the lands of the North, a rogue wolf in a well-worn deep blue uniform howled at the half moon, and five thousand howls and hoots and cries rang up in unison. And in the Shennan Valley, Míomar the wizard mouse pored over scrolls and peered into the blue flame of a hearth.

CONTINUED IN THE NEXT BOOK...

READ MORE MARCHWOOD...

Read the next book in the series for more cozy fantasy adventures in the forests of Marchwood.

Find out more about the mushroom folk called Strüm and learn the fate of Juniper and the sailing hares. Will Mother Elm help the Riverbank villagers?

In the West, will Nova and Foxy raise an army in the valley of the pine martens with the aid of Professor Woodruffe? Will Alumbrial send his forces in a siege on Riverbank Village? What about the rogue Wolf of the North, and the tales of Foxy's past? What portents will the mysterious mouse wizard bring to Marchwood? And what will Rudbeck request from the Toad King?

May your paws be warm and your fires be steady, my friends. Come back to Marchwood any time you need a fresh adventure, a happy feast, or a break from the wild world around you. We'll be here for you, deep in the woods, any time you like.

Find more books online at:

RALORENSEN.COM

R. A. Lorensen is a writer
from the Upper Peninsula of Michigan.

Sign up for new releases, news, and updates at
RALorensen.com.